A DIXIE MORRIS

DIXIE & SANDY

GILBERT MORRIS

MOODY PRESS
CHICAGO

To Mimi—
Your beauty and your meekness
grow more and more every day.
I love you!
Dixie

©1998 by
GILBERT MORRIS

All Scripture quotations, unless indicated, are taken from the *New American Standard Bible,* © 1960, 1962, 1963, 1968, 1971, 1972, 1973, 1975, 1977, and 1994 by The Lockman Foundation, La Habra, Calif. Used by permission.

ISBN: 0-8024-3366-9

1 3 5 7 9 10 8 6 4 2

Printed in the United States of America

CONTENTS

1

A SURPRISING REWARD

How do you like riding on old trolley cars, Dixie?"

Dixie Morris sat looking out the window of the green streetcar as it rumbled over the rails. The circus was in New Orleans, and Aunt Sarah had insisted on taking her on a tour of some of the historic sites. For the excursion Dixie had on a bright yellow dress with a rounded neck decorated with white roses in a raised puff print. She liked the dress. She thought it went well with her blue eyes and long blonde hair.

"It's nice, Aunt Sarah." She tried to smile.

Aunt Sarah, of course, had learned to know her niece very well since the two of them had joined the Royal Circus. She studied Dixie's face. "Are you worried about something? Something's wrong?"

Sarah's red hair and beautifully shaped green eyes caught the attention of almost everyone. She'd been delighted that, immediately after getting out of veterinarian school, she had landed a job as veterinarian for the Royal Circus. Dixie, living with Sarah while her parents were missionaries in Africa, enjoyed circus life, too.

But now she said, "I'm worried about Dolly."

"Dixie, you don't have to worry about either the gorilla or her baby."

"How do we know that they'll take good care of her at the Gorilla Institute?"

"That's their business, Dixie! Taking care of gorillas is what they do!" Sarah exclaimed.

Aunt Sarah and Dixie had taken care of a gorilla named Dolly as a favor to a friend. Then they found a baby gorilla whose mother had died, and they managed to obtain it for Dolly. And then Sarah had received a wire from the American Gorilla Institute saying that they had a place for Dolly and her baby.

Dixie's mouth turned down. "I don't

see why we couldn't have kept Dolly and Bonzo."

"It was just too hard, Dixie. The circus moves every week, at least. It wasn't good for Dolly and Bonzo to be hauled all over the country. At the Institute they'll get the very best care."

"Can we go visit them sometime?"

"Of course we can. Every time we're in the area, we'll go."

That cheered up Dixie somewhat, and when they reached the New Orleans zoo she had a great time. She especially wanted to see the tigers. "None of them is as nice as Stripes," she said.

Stripes was the Siberian tiger that was a special friend of Dixie's. Dixie and Stripes even appeared together briefly in the wild animal act directed by Val Delaney.

"They're not as pretty as Stripes, but then I bet you don't think any of the elephants are as nice as Jumbo, either, do you?"

"No. Jumbo was the nicest elephant in the world. I'd like to visit him and Chad sometime, too."

"Well, when the circus is in Arkansas, we'll be close to Chad's uncle's farm," Aunt

Sarah said. "I don't see why we couldn't take a little side trip. Do you think Jumbo will remember you?"

"Elephants never forget anything. He would never forget me!"

They went through the monkey house and laughed at the antics of the monkeys. Then they wandered through the rest of the zoo until Aunt Sarah said, "We'd better get back. We wouldn't want to miss the afternoon performance."

Dixie nodded, but she was not anxious to get back to the circus. She used to spend almost all her free time with Dolly and Bonzo, and now they were gone. "Now there's nothing to do," she complained.

This was not actually true. There was plenty to do at a circus. Both Dixie and her aunt stayed busy. They had made many friends, and both took part in the opening and concluding parades. They got to dress in glamorous costumes. Dixie liked her harem girl costume best. She thought she looked like Jeannie on the television program.

When they arrived at the circus grounds, she ran to the dressing tent and managed to be ready just as the parade started to form outside the Big Top.

"Hey, Dixie, I thought you were going to miss the Spec!"

"I'd never miss the parade!" Dixie called back to her friend Mickey. She stopped beside Ruth, and the elephant knelt so that Dixie could slip up on her back. She turned around to look at Mickey, who was riding Diane, his favorite elephant.

Mickey's father, Mooey Sullivan, was the big Irish elephant trainer. He was now grinning at Dixie, and his wife was smiling at his side. "Don't fall off," Mooey said, "and don't forget, you're coming to the church service tomorrow." Mr. Sullivan was also a preacher.

"I won't forget," Dixie said. She was always glad to see the Sullivans. She had become close friends with them.

The parade had just started when something hit her on the back. "Ow!" she said and looked around.

The Von Bulow horses, all mottled stallions, were right behind the elephants. On two of them rode the twins Eric and Marlene Von Bulow. They were ten, just Dixie's age. Eric was holding a small slingshot.

"I'll get you for that, Eric!" she said.

Eric merely laughed. He was a cocky

boy with blond hair and blue eyes. He was, Dixie thought, a real pain in the neck!

But Dixie enjoyed being in the parade. As it made its way around the inside of the Big Top, she waved at the spectators, and most of them waved back. Her costume was light blue and pretty. It made her feel exotic.

She had once told Mickey, her best friend, "That's what they wear in Arabia." But Mickey had said, "No, they don't. That's just in books and in movies."

But Dixie still believed that somewhere in Arabia there were girls who wore the kind of filmy costume that she did for the parade.

When the Spec was over, she saw Eric coming—probably to pinch her, she thought. His sister grabbed him by the hair and said, "Eric, leave Dixie alone!"

"Thanks, Marlene!" Dixie yelled and ran to change clothes again.

This time she put on a beautiful white dress and arranged her hair carefully in preparation for her tiger act. Then she waited, watching while the Castles did their high wire walk overhead. She had to admire Donald and Mrs. Castle. They were wonderful high wire walkers. Darla, their eleven-year-old daughter, was the most beautiful girl Dixie had ever seen. She'd been jealous when Darla had charmed Mickey for a time.

After the Castles, the ringmaster announced, "And now the most death-defying act on the continent! The Great Delaney and his Siberian tigers!"

Dixie watched Val, wearing white jodhpurs and a pure white shirt, enter the tiger cage. And then the cage was suddenly filled with beautiful Siberian tigers. They were all huge, almost white animals, much larger than Bengal tigers.

Dixie watched closely to see if Stripes, her favorite, did his tricks well. He did.

And then the ringmaster announced loudly, "And now Beauty and the Beast! Miss Dixie Morris will enter the cage with the eight-hundred-pound Siberian tiger! I ask for you to be quiet, ladies and gentlemen, for we all can see how dangerous this act is! Now, Miss Dixie Morris!"

Kirk, Val Delaney's younger brother, opened the steel door. He patted Dixie on the head and said, "Break a leg, Dixie."

Dixie laughed up at him, for he always said this. He told her it brought good luck.

"I will," she said. Then she entered the cage, and the spotlight came down on her. She walked right up to where Stripes was sitting on a low stool. Lifting a hand, she snapped her fingers and said, "Down, Stripes!"

The tiger came off the stool in that easy motion that all cats have. He walked to Dixie, who took him by the face and gave him a kiss. She liked it when a nervous laugh went over the crowd.

Then she said, "Time for our ride, Stripes!"

He growled deep in his throat and tried to lick her face.

Reaching into the small leather bag at her waist, where she always carried his chicken livers, she gave him one. "Do a good job, and you can have them all."

Easily she slipped onto his back, then said, "Now, here we go, Stripes. Around and around."

Stripes broke into a gentle lope, and they did go around and around the inside of the cage. The crowd applauded wildly.

Val Delaney stood close by all the time, his eyes watchful. He'd said that Stripes was the most trustworthy animal he had ever trained, but he was always careful. "All right, Dixie," he said. "Take your bows."

Dixie slipped off the tiger's back, gave him another handful of chicken livers, then curtsied. She loved the applause.

Leaving the cage, she went out to change her costume one last time. After that, she watched the rest of the acts and then rode Ruth, the elephant, in the final parade.

After the Spec wound out of the Big Top, Mickey came over to Dixie. He was a sturdily built boy, just her age, with bright red hair and light blue eyes. "I've got a present for you," he said rather shyly.

"What is it?"

"I'll come over to your trailer after while and give it to you."

"Good. Then we can maybe watch a movie."

She went back to the Airstream trailer that she shared with Aunt Sarah and removed the stage makeup from her face. It was fun putting on makeup for the performance. It was the only time she ever got to wear any.

She had just finished changing into

street clothes when a knock came at the door and Mickey stood at the step with a large box in his hands. He thrust it toward her. "Here it is. Your present."

"It's not my birthday," Dixie said.

"Well, I know that." Mickey seemed embarrassed. "But I made such a fool of myself with Darla Castle. You and I are best friends, and I didn't treat you very well."

"Well, you didn't have to buy me a present, but I'm glad you did. I love presents."

Dixie opened the box and took in a sharp breath. "Oh, Mickey, it's wonderful! Just what I wanted!"

"I know that." Mickey grinned. "It's all you've talked about for the last two weeks."

Dixie carefully lifted out the Barbie doll from the tissue paper. "It's Eliza Doolittle from *My Fair Lady*," she breathed. "Isn't she beautiful?" She held up the doll, and both of them admired it.

The doll was wearing a pink organza gown with a high neck, just like Eliza Doolittle's. She had on a matching hat with large ruffles around the brim. Dixie said, "Look, she's got a bow just like Eliza did. And pink shoes! She looks just like Eliza!"

"Well, if you're happy, I'm happy." Mickey was still grinning.

Dixie grinned. "I am. Come on. Let's make a place for her."

They went back to Dixie's section of the trailer. Her bedroom was small, and a great deal of it was taken up with her collection of Barbie dolls. Mickey, surprisingly enough, had taken an interest in her doll collection. He had taken a lot of ribbing from Eric Von Bulow over that but didn't seem to mind much anymore.

Still, something was on Dixie's mind, and after a while Mickey said, "What's the matter?"

"I got a letter from my folks. I can't go to be with them for a while longer. Living is hard there in Africa, and now there's an outbreak of cholera. They're afraid I'll get sick."

"That's too bad." Mickey leaned back and studied his friend. "Of course, I'd be sorry to see you go, but I know you miss your family. But look, you have to learn to take stuff like that."

"What do you mean?"

"I mean bad things happen. You get disappointed. You think everything's rotten." He suddenly grinned and ran his hands through his hair, making it stand straight up. "Then right after that maybe something really good happens. Just wait. Something good is going to turn up."

"I hope so." Dixie was doubtful. She did miss her parents. But then she smiled and said, "Something good did happen. You got me the nicest present I've had in a long time."

By the time Aunt Sarah came in, they were watching an old Shirley Temple movie on television.

"I've got good news for you, Dixie."

"What, Aunt Sarah?"

Sarah opened a drawer and pulled out an envelope. She was smiling. "This came today. It's from my friend Ada Shultz. She wants to reward us for taking such good care of Dolly for her."

"What is it?" Dixie asked curiously.

"It's two airline tickets."

"Where for?" Mickey asked with interest.

"For anywhere! They are round trip tickets for anywhere that the airline flies!"

"Do you see?" Mickey said, punching Dixie in the ribs. "I told you something good would happen."

"Where would you like to go?" Sarah asked.

Dixie thought, then said, "I'd like to go to England." She knew Aunt Sarah had talked about wanting to go to England.

"So would I," Sarah said. "We'll get some time off as soon as we can, and tally ho! Merry old England, here we come!"

2
A SAD
YOUNG LADY

Dixie watched with amusement as Russell Hamilton Bigg turned cartwheels. "That's good, Bigg," she said. "That'll go over great in your act."

"Clowns have to be funny. Sometimes I get tired of thinking up things to do."

The clown, being a midget, was not as tall as Dixie. He wore his tramp costume today. He had a red ball over his nose and big arched eyebrows, and he was wringing wet with sweat after his exercise. He sat beside Dixie on the grandstand and asked, "When are you and your aunt going for your vacation in England?"

"As soon as Aunt Sarah can work out something with Mr. Bennigen and Helen Langley." Bennigen was the road manager of the Royal Circus, and Helen Langley was his assistant.

Bigg said, "What made you want to go to England? You could go anywhere you wanted to."

"Well, I knew that's where Aunt Sarah wanted to go. It'll be fun."

After talking to Bigg for a while, Dixie said, "I've got to get back and clean up the trailer. See you later, Bigg."

"All right. Be careful. Don't take any wooden nickels." He always said that.

Dixie wandered back toward the Airstream. When passing Helen Langley's trailer, she saw the assistant manager at the door talking to an attractive, foreign-looking girl. She looked to be about eighteen and had olive skin and beautiful features. Her hair was so black that it seemed to be almost purple as it caught the sun.

Dixie was close enough to hear Miss Langley say, "I'm sorry, Aimee, but there's just no job I can give you."

Now, Dixie was a very curious girl. She lingered to hear what the dark-haired stranger would say.

"But I would be willing to do anything. Even clean up after the animals . . ."

Helen Langley had auburn hair. She was wearing jeans and a white, open-necked man's shirt. Dixie had always thought that she was very pretty.

Helen said regretfully, "I'm very sorry. Really, I am. If you had some sort of skill, that would be different. But there's just nothing right now for what you can do."

"Thank you very much, anyway, Miss Langley."

Helen went back into the trailer.

The dark-haired girl turned away so quickly that she bumped into Dixie. "Oh! I'm sorry!"

"That's all right," Dixie said. "It was my fault."

"Are you with the circus?"

"Yes. My aunt's the veterinarian."

"Oh, then you don't do an act."

"Well, actually I do. I ride a tiger around the ring."

The girl's eyes gleamed. "Then I saw you in the performance, but you looked different then. Much older."

Dixie grinned. She loved to be taken for an older girl. "That's because of the dress and all the makeup. I'm ten, actually." She hesitated, then said, "Do you live here in New Orleans? My name is Dixie Morris."

The girl smiled. "And my name is Aimee Feyd."

Dixie repeated the name. "What kind of name is that?"

"An Arab name. I come from the Middle East."

"Really?" Dixie thought of the harem girl costume she wore, and she said quickly, "I'd love to visit your part of the world."

"Not many visitors come where my family is. We spend much time far out in the desert."

Dixie thought she looked rather sad and also tired. "Do you work here in New Orleans?"

"I have been washing dishes in a cafe. It was all I could find. And then, two days ago, I lost my job."

Dixie was always sympathetic with people in trouble. She said, "I was going home and make myself a pizza. I make good pizzas. Why don't you come with me, Aimee, and you can help me eat it?"

"Oh, I can't do that."

"Sure, you can. That's our trailer right

over there. You'll like my Aunt Sarah. She's the veterinarian for the circus."

It took some persuading, but Dixie finally convinced the girl that it would be all right.

Aimee Feyd was impressed with how much larger the Airstream seemed inside than it did outside. Dixie took her on a tour of the trailer, showing her the stove, the small refrigerator, the table where she and Aunt Sarah ate, the bathroom, and the beds.

"And these are my dolls," she added proudly.

"They're very nice. I had dolls when I was a little girl." A cloud crossed Aimee's face.

Again, Dixie thought she seemed sad. She said quickly, "Maybe I'll just fix hamburgers. They're quicker than pizza. Do you like hamburgers?"

"Oh, I love American food. I've eaten many hamburgers."

Dixie went into the kitchen and took out the ground beef. She talked like a magpie, asking Aimee many questions about her country.

Aunt Sarah came in just as the hamburgers were done.

"Aunt Sarah, this is my new friend Aimee Feyd, and this is my Aunt Sarah, Aimee."

"I'm glad to know you, Miss Feyd."

"Oh, Aimee is fine. Your niece was kind enough to offer me a hamburger."

"She lost her job two days ago," Dixie said, "so I thought we would fix her up a nice supper."

"Well, you could've fixed something nicer than hamburgers!" Sarah said.

"Oh, I love hamburgers," Aimee said. "I love them with mustard and mayonnaise and pickle and onions or anything."

"Well, all right," Sarah said. "You two get it on the table, and I'll go wash up."

Dixie grilled more burgers, and the quick supper proved to be a wonderful success. Aimee ate two large hamburgers. And then Dixie heated some frozen blackberry cobbler.

"You must think I am a pig!" Aimee said, refusing another helping of cobbler. "But this was delicious."

She was a very pretty girl. She had enormous dark eyes and the smoothest complexion that Dixie had ever seen. Her dress was worn, though, and Dixie suspected she did not have many clothes.

"How did you get to America, Aimee?" she asked.

"Dixie, don't be so personal!" Aunt Sarah cried.

"Oh, it is all right." Aimee smiled at Dixie fondly. "Your niece is a very friendly young lady."

"She's a very nosy young lady!"

"I'm just interested in people," Dixie protested, "and I don't see anything wrong with asking how she got here."

Aimee took up the coffee cup that Dixie had put in front of her. "This is good coffee," she murmured. She sipped from it and then said, "It's not a very happy story. You would not be interested, I think."

"Of course, we would—if you'd want to tell it," Aunt Sarah said. "I've never been to the Middle East and don't know much about it. Do you have a large family there?"

"I have a father and mother, two brothers, and three sisters. My father is Sheikh Omar Feyd."

"Do you ride on camels and live in tents?" Dixie asked eagerly.

"Sometimes. Of course, there are cars

there, but my father doesn't like new things. He's very old-fashioned." Then she said softly, "I've been a great disappointment to him, I fear."

Dixie yearned to ask how that came about, but she knew her aunt would rebuke her for asking. Still, she couldn't hold back the questions. "Tell us more about where you lived, Aimee."

Dixie and Aunt Sarah sat quietly listening as the girl told them about life out in the desert. Her family raised goats and sheep and camels.

"I miss the camels. Especially one that was my favorite. He was almost pure white, and the name I gave him was Sandy."

"I never heard of a white camel," Dixie said. "I thought they were all brown."

"Well, white is rare, but he's very beautiful. I wish you could see him. He's smart too."

"I didn't know camels were smart," Dixie said.

"Sandy is, and many other camels are, too." Tears came to her eyes, and her lips trembled. "I miss Sandy very much, and I miss my family."

This time it was Sarah who asked a

question. "How long has it been since you've seen your family?"

"Six months now." She sighed. "You see, I became a Christian, and this displeased my father. Also I was in love with a young man who was a Christian. And although my father loves his family, he is a traditional Muslim. He said I could never see my family again."

"How awful," Sarah whispered.

"I had the money that I had saved all my life to go to school, and I sold my gold jewelry. I managed to get a job on a ship as a maid and came to the United States. At first, I thought that if I would get here, then Ahmed, my beloved, would come to me someday. But now I don't think that will ever happen."

Dixie put her hand on Aimee's shoulder. "It will be all right. God will take care of you."

Aimee seemed pleased at Dixie's words. She put her own hand over Dixie's. "That is what I have believed, but it is very hard."

Then she said, "I came to the circus because of the animals. I love animals, especially horses and camels." A puzzled look came into her eyes. "Our family raises racing camels. People in my country go to camel races as they go to horse races or dog races in this country. Why are there no trained camels in your circus?"

Aunt Sarah shook her head. "I don't know. Actually, I've never seen a trained camel."

"If I had Sandy here," Aimee said, nodding firmly, "I could train him. He was already so smart, and some of our other camels were, too. I saw the horses and the elephants doing their act today. Camels would make a good circus act." Then Aimee stood, saying, "It's been wonderful talking to you, and I thank you for the supper. The hamburgers were delicious."

Dixie said, "We have church tomorrow. Mr. Sullivan, the elephant trainer, is a preacher. Would you come?"

Aimee smiled shyly. "I would like that very much. What time?"

"At ten o'clock. And you don't have to dress up," Dixie added quickly, fearful that Aimee had nothing nice to wear. "Afterwards we can eat in the cook shack, and I'll take you around and show you all the animals up close, especially Stripes."

28

Aimee seemed very moved. "I've been wondering if I could continue in my life as a Christian. I had almost given up." Then she said, "Perhaps God put you in my way to encourage me."

Sarah put an arm around the girl. "All Christians must stick together. Don't give up hope. And we'll see you in the morning."

After Aimee left, Dixie said, "I just wanted to cry. Isn't it sad?"

"Very sad. It makes me think how ungrateful I am for all the good things we have."

Later that evening, when Aunt Sarah came in for their nightly prayers, they both prayed for Aimee. And later still, as Dixie lay holding the Eliza Doolittle doll, she whispered, "Lord, help Aimee. She's lonesome in a far country and away from her family. Take care of her. I ask it in Jesus' name. Amen."

Then she looked down at the doll and whispered, "It'll be all right, Eliza. You'll see."

3
DIXIE HAS A PLAN

I'm worried about Aimee," Dixie said.

She was watching Mickey wash the elephants with a garden hose. He was wearing his oldest pair of cutoffs and a white shirt with an emblem on the front that was so faded Dixie could not even recognize it. She herself had on a pair of blue jean cutoffs and a shirt with a large iguana on the front.

Mickey turned the hose into Ruth's mouth, and she gulped thirstily. "Elephants sure drink a lot of water," he said. After he finally got Ruth satisfied, he turned off the water and led her back to the rest of the herd. Then he returned to sit beside Dixie. He said, "I was surprised to see her come to church yesterday."

"I wasn't," Dixie said. "We'd invited her. She's a new Christian. It must be hard to be a Christian where there are no other Christians around."

"What are they where she lives?"

"Mostly Muslims, I think."

"What are *they?*"

"I don't really know. But she says there are Muslims all over the world. Her father's not sympathetic toward Christians from what she tells me."

"Well, we'll be leaving tomorrow, so she won't have a chance to come to the circus church anymore. Too bad."

Dixie was thoughtfully poking a stick in the dirt and kept silent for a time. Then she looked up. "Come with me, Mickey."

"Come on where?"

"We're going to go see Miss Helen."

"OK by me."

They made their way to Helen Langley's trailer, where they found her busy at her office desk.

Looking up, she smiled, saying, "What are you up to?"

"We've come to ask you a favor, Miss Helen."

"Well, what is it?"

"It's about Aimee Feyd."

"Aimee who?" Helen said with a puzzled look in her eyes.

"You know—the girl who was here asking for a job. She was at church yesterday. You remember?"

"Yeah, the good-lookin' one." Mickey grinned.

Dixie dug her elbow into his ribs. "Hush up, Mickey! This is serious!" Then she went on explaining to Miss Helen. "She really needs a job. She doesn't have any money and no place to go." She told some of the details of Aimee's life, while Helen leaned back in her chair and listened.

When Dixie finished, Helen Langley tapped her teeth with the eraser on her pencil and said, "Dixie, I wish I could help, but I don't know how I can. What could she ever do at a *circus*?"

"She's real smart, Miss Helen," Dixie said eagerly. "After church we went around, and I showed her the animals. Back home she took care of lots of animals—even camels."

"Well, we've got quite a bit of help now with the animals, and with your Aunt Sarah—"

"But you've forgotten, Miss Helen. We're

going on our trip soon. I know Aimee's not a veterinarian, but she could stay in our trailer and do some of the work with the animals. She knows how. Please? You don't have to pay her much. She doesn't have any place to go!"

Then Mickey threw himself into the argument.

After a while Helen said, "I'd forgotten about you two taking off on vacation. Well, come along. We'll talk to your aunt."

They found Sarah washing her hair. She put a towel around her head when they arrived, and she listened thoughtfully as Helen explained her problems.

Then Helen said, "You've met this girl. Do you really think she could be of any help?"

"Well, of course she's not a vet, but she's very quick to learn. Talk with her again, Helen. She's treated all kinds of goats and sheep and horses. Besides, I've got a lot of the animals on vitamins right now, and I'm not sure the handlers would always remember them. I think it might be wise to hire her to help out, at least temporarily."

"All right," Helen said. She turned to Dixie and smiled. "You're a persuasive young lady."

"And I'm a persuasive young man." Mickey grinned.

"She's coming to eat at the cook shack tonight," Dixie said. "We'll tell her then that the circus leaves tomorrow. I think she'll be ready."

The next day the circus moved on, and Aimee Feyd moved with it. Finding a place for her to stay until the Airstream was vacant was no problem. The cook, Clara Rendell, had an oversized trailer with an extra bed. She was a big, older woman with a voice louder than the roar of a full-grown lion, but she was also kindly, and she took Aimee under her wing.

Aimee proved to be a good worker. She was very smart, as Dixie had already known, and she threw herself into learning the routine of the circus. She also got a costume much like Dixie's and rode one of the Sullivan elephants in the Specs. She was not a bit afraid. She seemed to enjoy it, as a matter of fact.

On her third night with the circus, she came over to eat supper with Dixie and Sarah. Sarah had prepared pork chops, green beans, and mashed potatoes.

As they ate, Aimee told about what she ate in her homeland.

"Lots of goat. We love goat meat there. And cheese. Very strong sometimes. I do not think you would like it."

She helped wash the dishes, and afterward, when they were sitting around watching television, said, "I'm sure that God sent you two into my life." She had said this before, for she was a very grateful young lady. This time she added, "But I miss my family."

"I'll bet you miss Sandy the most of all the animals, don't you?" Dixie said.

"He was like a baby to me. I was there when he was born. He wobbled just like a young colt. But, oh, he was so smart. He's growing big now. I think about him every day."

Dixie asked little about Aimee's home, for she saw that it made the young woman sad.

The next day, she told Mickey all that Aimee had said. She tapped her chin with her finger.

Mickey said, "I know what you're doing. When you look like that and tap your chin, you're thinking."

"I think all the time!" Dixie protested.

"I mean you're hatching up some scheme. What's in that coco of yours?" He reached over and tapped her head with his knuckles.

"Ow, that hurts!" She shoved his hand away. "You know, if she just had Sandy here, and Ahmed, and if her family would love her in spite of her being a Christian, she'd be happy."

Mickey stared at her and shook his head in wonder. "You do think of a lot of things," he said.

"It's not a lot for God," Dixie insisted. "Aunt Sarah always says if two people agree on things—if they're good things—God will give it to them. Well, I think this is a good thing. Aimee is a new Christian, and she misses her sweetheart and her family and her camels, and she's sorry because her daddy's mad at her. Let's just pray that God would fix all that up."

Mickey scratched his head thoughtfully, but he finally said, "All right. It seems like a lot to me, though."

"It might be a lot for you, Mickey Sullivan, but nothing's too hard for God. We'll just pray about it, and you'll see."

4
JESUS CAN DO ANYTHING!

Circus life kept Dixie busy. She became so interested in Aimee Feyd that she almost forgot to grieve over Dolly's departure. From time to time she did think of the gorilla and her baby, but she realized now that it was best for them to be in a more stable place.

It became her joy to teach Aimee about circus life. One morning Aimee was watching the elephants rehearse, when she said to Dixie, "I understand about the elephants, and the tigers, and the horses, and all the other animals in the circus. But why is *he* here?"

Dixie looked to where Aimee was pointing. "Oh, that's Blinkey."

Blinkey was a small black and white dog with a shrill, yapping voice. He seemed to be everywhere.

Aimee was puzzled. "Who does he belong to?"

"I guess he just belongs to the whole circus," Dixie said. "When we first came, I wondered about that, too. He's not pretty, and he barks all the time. But I asked Bigg about it. He says every circus has to have a dog. You see, elephants and horses don't like anything under their feet, and sometimes, when there's a parade, a dog might get loose, and then the elephants would become afraid and run away. The same thing is true with Mr. Von Bulow's horses. They have to be very steady, you know, so that's where Blinkey comes in."

"That's his name? Blinkey?"

"Yes, and I don't know why. I've never seen him blink." Dixie shrugged. "Anyway, Bigg said that, with Blinkey around all the time, the horses and the elephants and the other nervous animals get used to noise and little animals around under them. So they won't be startled if a dog or a child gets close to them. So even Blinkey has a part in the circus."

"I think that's nice," Aimee said warmly. "He's a nice dog."

"You're still lonesome for your family and your animals, aren't you, Aimee?"

"Yes, of course. And I know you're lonesome for your parents, too."

Dixie knew her situation was not quite the same. She had Aunt Sarah, but Aimee had no one.

"Do you think you and Ahmed will ever get married?"

A sad look crossed Aimee's face. "I just don't see how it can be. He is so far away, and he has no money to come here. He's a fine young man. His family isn't wealthy, but, even so, my father would have accepted him as a son-in-law if Ahmed had not become a Christian. But now, Father will never agree to our marrying."

"I wish I could meet Ahmed. I'll bet he's handsome."

"He is," Aimee said, her eyes brightening. "He's very handsome. He's tall, and he has the neatest beard, and his skin is like copper. Oh, he's the handsomest man I've ever seen!" She went on to talk about Ahmed, but finally she sighed. "I may never see him again." She rose and walked off quickly, and Dixie thought she had seen tears gathering in her eyes.

Dixie thought often about Aimee that day, and that night after supper she said, "Aunt Sarah, I've been thinking a lot."

Aunt Sarah was washing dishes. She turned and looked at Dixie with her eyebrows lifted. "I always get nervous when you say that. What scheme have you got cooked up this time?"

"It's not a scheme," Dixie said. "It's just something that makes sense."

"Well, let's have it. It can't be any wilder than some of your other ideas."

"You know the tickets that Mrs. Shultz sent us to go on a vacation?"

"Of course. Are you anxious to get to England?"

Dixie had thought this over very carefully, and now she sprang her surprise. "Let's go to the Middle East instead of England, Aunt Sarah."

"Why in the world would you want to go to the Middle East? Oh, I know. It has something to do with Aimee, doesn't it?"

"Yes, we could go see her family, and maybe we'll meet her boyfriend, Ahmed. And her father may like us and not be mad at Aimee anymore."

"That's a wild idea even for you. If he

wouldn't forgive his daughter, why should he listen to two strangers?"

Dixie was frowning with concentration. "Maybe he would even give her Sandy as a present, and maybe Ahmed could come back to America with us and get a job with the circus."

"Wait a minute, Dixie! Don't always be dreaming those dreams. You think everything's like a storybook."

"But you said in Sunday school last Sunday that nothing was too hard for God."

Sarah dried her hands on a towel. Then she came over and put her arm around Dixie and hugged her. "You have a very generous nature, Dixie. You want everything to come up nice for everyone, and I think that's wonderful. But this just doesn't sound likely."

"Well, we've got the tickets, and you remember the verse that you had me memorize —about all things working together for good to the people who love the Lord. Do you remember that?"

"I remember it, of course—"

"Well, maybe we got the tickets just so we could go see Aimee's family, and maybe it'll all work out for good for Aimee."

Finally Sarah said, "Let's go talk to Mooey Sullivan. He knows about the Bible and getting guidance as well as anybody."

They found Mooey and Mrs. Sullivan sitting in front of their trailer. Mickey was there, too, reading a book as usual. He loved books more than anyone else Dixie had ever seen!

"Well, this is a surprise," Mr. Sullivan said. "Let me drag out a couple of chairs." He found two lightweight aluminum chairs, and the two visitors were soon seated.

Sarah said, "Dixie has an idea, Brother Sullivan, and we want to see what you think about it."

Mooey Sullivan and his family listened as Sarah explained. She ended by saying, "I told her that it's very unlikely that anything would ever come of it. She's become very fond of Aimee, and so have I, but it just doesn't seem probable that her father would forgive her."

"But we won't know until we try!" Dixie piped up. "Isn't that right, Mr. Sullivan?"

Mooey Sullivan bobbed his head. "No, we never know until we try. But it's one thing to be impulsive and jump off into deep water, and it's another thing to act when God tells us to."

"But how are we going to know the difference?"

"Pray and ask that God show us. I always think if there's a door open, God could have opened it. And since the tickets have come and your trip would be free, maybe that indicates an open door."

"That's what I said!" Dixie exclaimed. "You see, Aunt Sarah! Mr. Sullivan wants us to go."

Laughing, Mooey held up his hand. "I didn't say that. I said we'd have to pray about it."

"Mickey and I have already been praying about it, haven't we, Mickey?"

"That's right, Dad. Just like you always preach at us. If two of us agree, and God thinks it's a good thing, it's gonna to be done."

Mr. Sullivan said, "In a situation like this —when I'm not quite sure of what to do—I start moving toward what seems to be right. Then, if I don't get a red light, I go for it. If I get a red light, I stop and say, 'Well, that wasn't God's plan.'"

"Let's all pray then," Dixie said. And they did.

The circus was like one big family. Although the families lived in their own trailers, there were very few secrets.

The day after Dixie and Sarah talked to the Sullivans, Eric Von Bulow and Darla Castle were practicing in the arena, and Dixie and Mickey were watching. Darla was doing her high wire act, and she did a marvelous job. She actually did a dance on the wire. Her father sat on the ground below, directing her.

"She's so graceful," Dixie said. "I can't even walk across a bridge without getting dizzy, and look at her."

Mickey shrugged. "Well, she's been doing it all her life."

When Darla came down, she and Eric joined Dixie and Mickey. They both were grinning.

"We heard about what you want to do, Dixie," Darla said. "You want to go all the way to Arabia or someplace."

Neither Darla nor Eric was a Christian, and they frequently made fun of Dixie and Mickey's praying and studying the Bible.

"You'd just be wasting your time," Eric said. "I know what those Arabs are like. Her dad's not going to bend, not one inch."

"You don't know that," Mickey said.

"What do you mean, I don't know it? Of course I know it!" Eric always thought he was right. "You watch what I tell you. You'll go over there, and nothing will come of it, and you'll waste your whole vacation."

"That's right." Darla sniffed. She held her nose in the air in a way that irritated Dixie and said, "If I were you, I'd forget all about visiting that girl's family."

Dixie stared at them and said, "Well, I've got a dream that it'll all come out all right."

"That's what you are. Just a dreamer," Darla said. "You need to face up to reality, Dixie. Let's go, Eric." She motioned to him, and they walked off.

Dixie's feelings were hurt. "I guess she's right about me being a dreamer."

Mickey looked at her. "That's what they said about Joseph in the Bible, and he came out all right. He ruled all the land of Egypt."

Dixie laughed. "Well, I don't want to rule all of Egypt. Or all of any country. I just want Aimee to get her sweetheart, and get her camel, and get her family to love her."

47

Two days after that, Sarah suddenly said, "I think it would be a good thing for us to take a trip to the Middle East after all. We may not do any good, but we can try. And at least we can see how her people live."

"Oh, that's wonderful! Let's go tell Aimee."

Aimee Feyd was so excited that she almost jumped up and down. "And you will see my family!" she exclaimed. "You will tell them that I am all right. That I am working in a circus with you."

"We'll try to see Ahmed too. What will we tell him?"

A flush came into the girl's cheeks. "We do not speak so easily of love and things like that as you Americans. I will write him a letter."

Sarah smiled. "I think that might be best."

"When will you be going?"

"As soon as we can get things tidied up," Sarah said. "I'll go tell Ace Bennigen and Helen right away to get ready to do without us for a couple of weeks."

As soon as Sarah was gone, Aimee threw her arms around Dixie. She was very strong, and she swung Dixie around easily.

"This is all your doing, Dixie. If you had not found me and taken me home with you, it would never have happened."

Dixie was pleased that Aimee was happy. "Now, tell me everything about your family, so that when I meet them it'll be just like I know them all."

She sat down, and Aimee talked about her mother and brothers and sisters but mostly about her father. She ended by saying, "He is such a good man, so kind. But he is very upset with me, and that grieves me very much." Then she brightened and said, "But God is going to do something, isn't He?"

"He sure is," Dixie said, nodding firmly. "You pray here, and we'll go to see your family."

"And when you see Sandy, put your arms around him and tell him that his Aimee misses him very much."

"I've heard that camels spit on people," Dixie said cautiously. "He wouldn't do that, would he?"

"My Sandy? Of course not. He's very loving. You just put your arms around him, and you'll see."

"All right. I'll try it, but I never kissed a camel before."

49

The airport terminal was crowded, and the air was filled with the sound of people talking and loudspeakers making announcements.

"You must be careful when you get to my country. Things will be very different there."

"Oh, I'm sure they will be, Aimee." Sarah smiled at her. "I've never been any place like that, but I've seen pictures in magazines."

"Pictures in magazines are not the same," Aimee warned. "It is a different world, my home."

Dixie stopped by a newsstand to buy a magazine, then asked, "Isn't it time to get on the airplane, Aunt Sarah?" she asked.

"Yes, they just made the boarding

announcement." Sarah kissed Aimee on the cheek. "Pray for us that we will find favor with your family, Aimee."

"Oh, I have already been doing that." Aimee returned the kiss, then bent over and embraced Dixie. "You are going to love my sister Zilla. She's the same age as you are and very lively—just as you are, Dixie."

Dixie's eyes were bright. She was so excited about the trip that she shifted her feet eagerly. "I'll do what you said about Sandy."

"Yes, be sure you give him a good hug. You'll love him too, Dixie. I know you love all animals."

Dixie had her doubts, for she had a notion that camels were nasty, ill-tempered beasts. She did not want to hurt Aimee's feelings, however, so she just smiled and said, "I'll give him an extrahard hug just for you."

"Let's go, Dixie. We must get on the plane. Good-bye, Aimee."

Dixie said, "Good-bye," and then they hurried to the door that led to the plane. They walked down a long, narrow corridor, the flexible gateway that went all the way to the front door of the huge airplane.

When they stepped inside and turned into the body of the plane, Dixie gasped. "It's so big!"

"Yes, this is a jumbo jet."

Dixie's eyes went everywhere as they moved down one of the two aisles. "It's kind of like a theater."

"A little bit."

The plane was divided into three sections. The middle section was very wide and had about fifteen seats. On each side were smaller sections of five seats each. Dixie was quick to notice that the length of the plane was divided so that each section had its own TV screen.

"Here are our seats, right here. You have the one by the window. Isn't that nice?"

Dixie plumped down in her seat, and then they waited for the plane to take off. Dixie watched the cabin fill up as all kinds of people got on. Some were dark skinned and some were light skinned. She saw one oriental family, a man and a woman with three children, including a small baby. Several women wore dresses down to their shoes, and headdresses, and veils.

"They must be going to the Middle

East. They dress like the ladies in the pictures we saw," Dixie whispered.

Finally the big plane rolled out on the runway, and Dixie was thinking, *I don't see how anything this big ever gets up in the air.*

Nevertheless, the plane did take off, surging upward with such power and speed that it caught her breath. She watched the earth fall away until finally the terminal looked like a toy building. They flew through clouds, which delighted Dixie, and then the pilot said, "We are now cruising at thirty thousand feet. Enjoy your flight."

Dixie watched the clouds form a solid, white mass below the plane. "It looks like you could fall into them like into cotton, doesn't it, Aunt Sarah?"

"Well, I don't think it would be quite like that. We came up through them. In a way, it's like going through steam."

For a time Dixie was fascinated by the cloud formations, but after a while she grew restless. "Can I listen to the music on the earphones, Aunt Sarah?"

"Of course, you can."

Dixie found the magazine that listed the different stations. Some were country western, some were rock and roll, others were of still different types of music. She put on the earphones, found a station, and listened with delight.

On other flights, all they had been given to eat were a package of peanuts and a Coke, but when this plane had been in the air for two hours, the attendant came along and brought full meals.

"Look, Aunt Sarah, it's some kind of chicken. A baby one, I think."

"It's a full-grown chicken. It's what's called a Cornish hen," Aunt Sarah said. "That's as big as they get. And I see we get English peas, mashed potatoes, a salad, and dessert too."

Dixie happily ate the chicken. The legs were so tiny that she could eat them in one bite. "They're very small drumsticks, but it's good."

"Very good. We'll get plenty to eat on this flight. It's a long one."

The big plane droned on and on. When it grew dark, a movie came on. It was not a movie that Dixie particularly liked, but she watched it nevertheless. Finally she grew sleepy, and Aunt Sarah said, "Put your seat back, and we'll put one of the blankets over you, and you can take a good nap."

"All right, Aunt Sarah," Dixie said. She was very tired, and she went to sleep almost at once.

Dixie awoke when the sunlight streamed through the window and hit her face. She sat up and rubbed her eyes.

"We're landing soon, Dixie. We're in London."

"Are we almost to Aimee's country?"

"Oh, no. That's still a long way. We get to stay overnight here and see some of the sights."

Dixie and Aunt Sarah visited as many places in London as they could. They went to see the Changing of the Guard at Buckingham Palace, and Dixie wondered at the tall soldiers in their scarlet uniforms and high helmets. After the guard was changed, she and Aunt Sarah walked by one of the uniformed men, and Dixie said, "Hello. My name is Dixie. What's yours?"

"He can't talk to you. Dixie. They are trained not to react in any way. No matter what you do, he won't speak, or smile, or laugh, or anything else."

Dixie stared at the handsome, tall soldier and said, "I bet I can make him laugh." She made faces and did other silly things, but the soldier's expression did not flicker. He might as well have been made of marble.

Sarah laughed at Dixie's disappointment. "Come along, Dixie. We only have the one day to see things."

They visited other important places, including the National Museum of Art and the house where Charles Dickens had lived. When they finally went to bed, Dixie slept hard until the next morning.

Again Dixie was fascinated as the plane took off. She found she was still not too tired of traveling to enjoy the flight. She noticed that many more Arab people had gotten on in London. Now it seemed most of the people in the plane were of that nationality.

"What's the name of the place we're going, Aunt Sarah?"

Aunt Sarah told her. "Well, we land at an international airport, but Aimee's family lives at a smaller place out in the desert. We'll have to find them."

"That's a strange name."

"Well, I guess people from here would think that Cincinnati was a funny name—or Toad Suck Ferry."

Dixie laughed aloud. "There's no place such as Toad Suck Ferry!"

"Yes, there is. It's a little place in Arkansas. I've been there."

"I'd hate to live *there*," Dixie decided. "I wouldn't want to tell anybody I lived in Toad Suck Ferry!"

In midafternoon, the pilot announced their landing approach, and the plane began to descend.

When Dixie could see the land below, she cried, "It looks like a *desert* down there!"

"That's what most of this country is, Dixie. There are very few trees, or rivers, or lakes."

Dixie watched as the plane went down lower and lower and finally landed on a long strip of tarmac. She unfastened her safety belt and followed Aunt Sarah when the plane unloaded. As soon as they stepped outside, Dixie gasped. "It's so *hot!*"

"Yes, we're nearer the equator now. Closer to the sun," Aunt Sarah said. "We'll have to put on our coolest clothes. These will be too hot."

Dixie was stunned by the babble of voices. She heard almost no one speaking English. Most of the people who had gotten off the plane were Arab, and all of the officials talked in Arabic. She found they spoke English too, though, and finally she and Aunt Sarah got through Customs and gathered their baggage.

"We'll have to find a hotel," Aunt Sarah said. "Then we'll get transportation to find the Feyd family."

Stepping outside the terminal, Dixie saw a string of unfamiliar-looking taxis. But mostly she was looking at the people. Very few of the women were dressed as she and Aunt Sarah were. Most wore long, dark dresses that touched the earth, and many of them wore black coverings on their faces.

"I'd hate to have to wear an outfit like that," she said. "You'd think they'd burn up."

"I suppose they're used to it," Sarah said. She was looking around hesitantly, when a short, rather chubby young man wearing a chauffeur's cap stepped up. "I speak English good," he announced with a broad smile. "May I take you somewhere?"

"We need to find a hotel for the night," Sarah said.

"Ah, yes. How much you want to pay? A whole lot? Not much?"

"Somewhere in the middle, I suppose."

"Then the Hotel Yussif. You will like that. Many Americans stay there. You are from America? Yes?"

"Yes, we are, and the Hotel Yussif will be fine."

"Good. I take your baggage. My name is Benji."

Benji hustled to get their baggage loaded into his ancient cab, and then he opened the door for them. There was no air conditioning, and the heat was stifling.

Benji drove down several crooked streets, while his passengers stared out at the city.

It was so different from an American city! Dixie saw several modern buildings, but soon they were in an older part of town where the buildings were not high. Many of these had turrets on top, such as she had seen pictured in magazines. And the people that crowded the streets looked very different from any she had ever seen in the States.

The cab stopped in front of a white, three-story building with potted plants in front.

"Here, the Hotel Yussif," Benji said, and he opened the door and waved toward the building. "I will get your luggage."

Soon Benji had gotten the bags together and carried them into the lobby, where a dark-skinned man with a thin mustache and wearing a white suit greeted them with a smile. "Welcome to the Hotel Yussif. Will you be staying long, madam?"

"No, just overnight."

"If you will sign here, you will have a fine room."

Aunt Sarah signed the register, then said, "I will be needing to go to a village called Afif tomorrow. Can you tell me the best way to get there?"

The tall man shrugged his shoulders expressively. "That will not be easy. Afif is a small place, you understand. No planes or trains go there."

"So how can we get there?" Aunt Sarah asked.

"There is a bus. It will be crowded, but

it is the only way. It leaves in the morning at nine."

Benji had been standing by, listening. "I will pick you up," he offered, "and take you to the bus station."

"Oh, that's very nice of you. We'll be waiting."

The room that they were given was small but clean. It was on the third floor, and Dixie watched out the window until dark, fascinated by the city sights.

In the morning, Dixie and her aunt dressed quickly, then went downstairs.

"Where might we get breakfast?"

"There is a small cafe right next to the hotel. The food is very inexpensive," the room clerk said.

As Dixie walked along with Aunt Sarah, she noticed that many people stared at them. They were wearing cooler clothes today, just lightweight dresses. Aimee had warned them not to wear shorts, for that would be offensive to the Arab people.

Unfortunately, breakfast was not what Dixie had been accustomed to. The main item was some sort of fish, and she did not like fish for breakfast. There was porridge too, something like oatmeal, and an egg.

When they left the cafe, Sarah said, "I think I'm going to lose weight on this trip. I'm not used to this kind of food."

They saw Benji waiting outside the hotel, his teeth gleaming in a smile. He helped them load their bags and then drove to the bus station. It was a primitive affair, and the bus itself was old and had lost most of its paint.

"Do you think this can make it to Afif?" Aunt Sarah asked doubtfully.

"It may break down a few times," Benji acknowledged, "but it will get you there."

Aunt Sarah smiled wryly and paid the cab driver. Then she purchased tickets for Afif.

When they got on the bus, Dixie was shocked. It was packed full, not only with people but with several animals. One woman held a cage with two roosters in it. Another family had a large dog that barked continually. Most dramatic of all was a big goat that kept making odd sounds.

"I never thought I'd be sharing a bus with a goat," Aunt Sarah said, shaking her head. "But it will be all right."

The ancient vehicle finally started up and rattled down the road and out of the city. Looking out the window, Dixie was a little frightened. The road had quickly become simply a rough dirt track, winding around rocks and past scrub vegetation. Overhead the sky was a very pale blue-gray. It looked hard enough to strike a match on.

"There's just nothing out here, Aunt Sarah," she whispered.

About that time the goat came down the aisle, and Dixie made the mistake of giving him a piece of candy. After that, he continually nudged her for the rest of the journey until he had gotten all the candy that she had.

The sun climbed high, and the inside of the bus became hot as an oven. Sweat ran down Dixie's face, and her dress was saturated, as was Aunt Sarah's. They had not thought to bring drinking water, and soon Dixie's mouth was dry. One time the bus stopped at a small village consisting merely of a dozen shacks, but at least they were able to buy some soft drinks there.

"I'm afraid to drink any of the water. It might make us sick," Sarah said. She bought as many soft drinks as they could carry, and they drank the sweet mixtures thirstily.

All day long the bus rolled on and on. About sundown they came to Afif, and Dixie and her aunt got off, stiff, sweat-stained, and weary.

"I'd been hoping we would find someone here who can speak English," Sarah said. "But it doesn't look very likely."

However, the small town of Afif did have a few English-speaking people. The rather dirty inn was run by a man and wife who listened as Sarah explained that she was looking for a family named Feyd.

"Ah, yes." The owner nodded. He was round and had a shiny, moon-shaped face and small eyes. "The sheikh, you mean."

"I suppose so. His name is Omar Feyd."

"Yes. The sheikh. He is not in Afif just now. He owns a house here, but he is out with his family in the desert with their flocks."

Aunt Sarah looked so tired she could hardly stand up. "How could we get to him?"

"Stay the night here," the innkeeper advised. "Tomorrow I will help you find someone who can guide you to Sheikh Omar."

"Thank you very much. We would like a room."

That night was hard on both visitors. There was no bathroom except for one down the hall. The little hotel was full, so they had to wait for a considerable time before getting their baths.

When they finally lay down on the lumpy mattress, Dixie whispered, "I hope there are no bedbugs."

"So do I," Sarah said. "But this may be the last bed we get for some time, so you'd better enjoy it!"

6
DIXIE MEETS A RUDE CAMEL

After a sleepless night, Dixie and Aunt Sarah hastily took advantage of the early hour to have a shower. The air was already warm by the time they had dressed and gone downstairs to find the innkeeper.

"Have you found someone to take us to Sheikh Omar?"

"My nephew. He is a trustworthy young man." He hesitated, then said, "It is not altogether safe to travel so far into the desert, especially for women. The Feyds travel with their flocks, and no one knows exactly where they will be today or tomorrow. But my nephew, for a time he served as a herdsman for the sheikh. He can find him if anyone can, and he is very responsible."

"That's all right," Aunt Sarah said

quickly. "I would want to pay him a fair wage. Could we get breakfast first?"

Breakfast included pancake-shaped bread with strange butter to spread on it. Dixie asked, "What kind of butter is this?"

"I think it may be goat butter. It has a strong taste, doesn't it?"

"I'm going to cover it up with this jam. Maybe it'll kill the taste."

The jam seemed to be made of figs and was very good. There were also raisins and some kind of melon and strong, thick coffee, which neither Dixie nor Aunt Sarah could drink.

"I don't see how they drink this," Sarah said. "It's so strong."

"I wish I had some Ovaltine, but I don't guess there's any of that in this place."

After breakfast and a wait of nearly an hour, the innkeeper came to find them. "My nephew is here. I have told him that you can work out his wages."

Dixie and Sarah looked up to see a young man approaching. He was thin and tall. He wore a robe, and a red and white cloth covered his head.

"He looks like a desert sheikh, doesn't he?" Dixie whispered.

"I don't think he's a sheikh," Sarah whispered back.

"My name is Yussif," the man said and bowed deeply. "My uncle tells me you wish to find Sheikh Omar."

"Yes. Can you take us to him?"

"You are acquainted with the sheikh?"

"We are good friends with his daughter."

"Ah, Sheikha Aimee." Yussif nodded. "Yes, I knew her well when I worked for the sheikh."

"When can we leave?"

"It is at your pleasure, but first we must make financial arrangements. It may be expensive for you," Yussif said. "There are my wages and transportation expenses, and no man can say how soon we will find Sheikh Omar. You understand that they have flocks. They travel where there is grazing."

"Yes, I understand that. What do you think would be a fair amount for your services?"

Sarah and the Arab bargained, and when arrangements were made, Yussif said, "We can leave now, but . . ." He looked at their clothes. He shook his head. "It will be difficult in those clothes."

"What should we wear, Yussif?"

The question seemed to puzzle the man. He stroked his chin thoughtfully and shook his head. "If you were of my people, you would wear a long dress with a covering for your head and your face. But you have nothing like that, I suppose."

"No, we don't. We just have American dresses."

"I have seen in American movies that some American women wear trousers such as men wear."

"Yes, we have some of those. They are called slacks. Are those all right?"

"Our people would not permit it. But since you are Americans and strangers . . . yes, that would be more suitable."

"We'll change right away," Sarah said.

They went back to their room and changed into cotton slacks, light, long-sleeved blouses, and sandals. Aimee had warned that this might happen, and she had suggested they bring along such garments. They also had sun helmets and plenty of sunscreen. Aimee had also warned that they would burn badly if they did not take proper care.

After they had applied the sunscreen

liberally to their hands, faces, and necks, they went outside and found Yussif waiting. They had expected that he would have a car or perhaps a truck. He did not.

"We're going to have to ride on *those?*" Dixie exclaimed, staring at the five camels that stood chewing their cud.

"It is the only way. You have never ridden a camel?"

"I've ridden an elephant . . ."

Yussif stared in astonishment, then he smiled. His teeth were very white against his bronze skin. And then he laughed aloud. "If you have ridden an elephant, then a camel should not be difficult. Come. I will show you how to mount."

Aunt Sarah mounted her camel with little difficulty. The beast seemed to be patient and gave no trouble.

However, when Yussif motioned Dixie forward, he said, "This camel is very stubborn. I keep him because he is tough and tireless, but he has a will of his own. Down there, you stubborn beast!"

Dixie was standing beside Yussif as he tapped the camel's leathery, front knees. The camel uttered a groan that sounded like metal rubbing against metal. Then, without warning, he turned and spit at Dixie!

Dixie screamed. She grabbed for her handkerchief. She heard Yussif shouting at the camel in Arabic. She heard Aunt Sarah crying, "Dixie, are you all right?"

"I guess so," Dixie said, wiping her face with a shudder. "He spit right in my face!"

Yussif was apologetic. "I struck him on the nose. He shouldn't do it again."

"I don't want to ride that awful beast!"

Yussif shook his head sorrowfully. "I'm sorry, but there is no other way. Once you get on his back, it will be all right. I would let you ride one of the others, but they do not ride as easily. They are mostly for carrying baggage."

Dixie looked with despair at Aunt Sarah, who could only say, "I guess you'll have to do it, Dixie."

"All right," she said grimly.

Yussif made the camel kneel. "His name is Loti, which means 'stubborn' in my language."

Dixie waited until Loti had knelt, and then quickly slipped into the saddle. It was actually very comfortable. Loti lurched upward, and she felt very far from the ground. The camel turned and looked her in the eye, and Dixie tapped him on the nose. "Don't you dare spit at me, you awful creature!"

Loti uttered a mournful groan.

Then Yussif mounted his camel and said, "Now, we will go."

As she began swaying back and forth in the saddle, Dixie said to herself, *This trip isn't going to be as much fun as I thought!*

Still, riding a camel was not too bad. These animals had a slow, plodding gait, but Aimee had told her that racing camels could cover the ground at an astonishing rate.

They traveled steadily for two hours, and then Yussif pulled up the camels in a grove of palm trees. They had reached an oasis. They dismounted and stretched their legs while Yussif watered the animals.

Then, as they rested, Yussif told them a little about camels. "They are marvelous for the desert," he said. He sat with legs crossed under him in the shade of a palm. He had filled the canteens, and they were eating some of the sweet cakes that he had bought for provisions. "Horses sink down in the deep sand, so desert travel is very hard for them. But the camel has a broad foot and walks on top of the sand."

"I've heard they can go for a long time without water," Sarah commented.

"Yes, that is true. Far longer than any human. They store it up and can go for days without more. The same is true of food."

"Is the food and water in their hump?" Dixie asked.

"That is true."

"If only they wouldn't spit on people."

Yussif laughed. "You will never make a friend of Loti. Camels are often temperamental and stubborn. If they decide not to go on, then nothing can make them. But that usually happens when they haven't been fed or had enough water or rest. We'll have no trouble—except with Loti, who seems to be more than usual a camel who knows his own mind."

Dixie would always remember wandering around in the desert looking for Sheikh Omar. The blistering sun seemed to suck the energy out of her, and she grew very tired. At night she gladly fell asleep in the little tent that Yussif put up for her and

Aunt Sarah. They always stopped near some small oasis settlement where they could buy food, but there was nothing like an inn available.

Sarah was careful to keep them both liberally anointed with sunscreen. "I don't know what would happen if people didn't do this," she said. One time she'd forgotten to put sunscreen on the side of her neck, and it had turned rosy almost at once.

"This is an awful place to live," Dixie said. "I'd hate to live here forever. I don't see how people stand it."

"I don't suppose they think it's awful," Sarah replied. "People pretty much like what they get used to."

On the third day, Yussif stopped to ask some herdsmen for news of Sheikh Omar. When he came back to the camels, a smile was on his face.

"We have good fortune. By nightfall we should find the sheikh. They are over there." He pointed across the trackless sand and then mounted his camel. "We will go faster now, for I want to find their camp before dark."

Dixie had to hang on. At first the quicker pace was fun, but later she became so tired she had to hold on just to keep from falling off.

When it was almost dusk, Yussif cried, "There are the tents of Sheikh Omar and his people!"

Dixie looked down into a valley and saw some greenery. Apparently, there was a spring or perhaps a stream. She saw tents spread over a considerable area. Many were pure white. Others were red, and still others were dark, almost black.

Yussif urged the camels forward.

Dixie hung onto the saddle as Loti broke into a gallop.

"They have seen us coming. There is the sheikh," Yussif called out.

Their guide drew the camels to a halt by the tents and came off his mount easily. He bowed deeply to a tall man wearing a white robe, spoke something Dixie could not understand, and then said in English, "I have brought visitors, my honored Sheikh. They do not know Arabic."

"These have come to see me?"

Dixie was surprised at the sheikh's good use of English.

"They are friends of your daughter in America. This is Sarah Logan and her niece, Dixie Morris." He motioned to the sheikh and said, "This is Sheikh Omar Feyd."

Aunt Sarah stepped forward. She said, "I do not know your customs, but I am honored to meet you, Sheikh Omar."

"Me too," Dixie said. She studied the man. He had a lean, fierce look. His black beard was streaked with silver. His eyes were penetrating. His face reminded her of a hawk.

"You have come from America?"

"Yes," Sarah said. "We have grown to be good friends with your daughter, and we bring you greetings from her."

The sheikh's face did not change.

Then a woman came up beside him. She wore no face covering, but she did wear the long, full costume of the local Arab women. "You have seen my daughter?" she asked. She had a softer manner than her husband. "You have seen our Aimee?"

"This is my wife, Fatima," the sheikh said. He did not wait for more talk but said, "You will be our guests." He clapped his hands, and instantly a small, wizened man with a silver beard stepped forward. "See to it that they have comfortable lodging and water for bathing," he commanded. "And prepare a meal."

"At once, Sheikh Omar."

The sheikh turned away, but Fatima whispered, "I am glad you have come."

"Thank you, Fatima," Aunt Sarah said. "We have much to tell you."

The old man showed them to a tent that was fairly large. The sand floor was covered with Persian rugs, and although there were no chairs, there were many thick cushions. Gratefully, they washed in the water that was brought in large pots.

Then a servant spread a plastic cloth on the floor and brought in a huge tray of meat served over rice. It was probably goat, Aunt Sarah said, but Dixie thought it was delicious.

Both Dixie and her aunt were exhausted and gladly got ready for bed. Before Dixie went to sleep, she said, "Mr. Omar looks stern, doesn't he?"

"Yes, he does." Sarah's voice was sleepy sounding. "I don't think it's going to be easy to convince him to forgive his daughter."

7
A MAD DAD

Dixie stuck her head outside the tent flap. The sun was barely visible over the horizon, and the tents made shadows on the desert sand. Dixie thought, *I wish it would stay this cool all day—but it won't.*

"We'd better get dressed, Aunt Sarah."

Her aunt was still not quite awake. But she stirred and sat up, moving her shoulders stiffly. "Sleeping on the sand isn't too bad," she said. "But I miss my innerspring mattress."

"So do I, but I guess we'll get used to it."

"I don't know," Sarah said as she stood up carefully and arched her back. "I'm not sure how long we'll be here. Sheikh Omar didn't seem very happy to see us."

"He looks mean to me. But Aimee said

he was a nice man, except when he doesn't get his own way."

"I suppose all of us are a bit like that." Sarah managed a smile. "We need to wash our clothes. They are so sweaty, but I'm not sure there's water enough for that."

They dressed hurriedly, but by the time they stepped outside, the sun was a huge pale ball in the east. Already the heat from it was obvious, and Dixie knew it would be a very hot day.

A woman approached them and bowed deeply. She spoke no English but motioned with her hand for them to follow her.

"I wish I could understand Arabic," Dixie said.

"So do I. It would make things much easier. I'm glad at least the sheikh and his wife speak such wonderful English. Obviously, they are very Westernized. Well, let's go. She wants us to follow."

They went with the woman to the largest tent, a snow-white one made of a lightweight material. The lower part of the tent had been lifted so that what little breeze there was could blow through. They stepped inside.

Fatima advanced and bowed. "Welcome to our home." She was wearing a gray robe and a head covering that was tied back from her face. She had a strong face, and Dixie could see the resemblance between her and her daughter.

"This is my daughter Zilla."

Zilla was a small girl with almond-shaped brown eyes and a wiry aspect. She murmured something in Arabic to which her mother said, "Speak English, Zilla."

"Hello," Zilla said to Sarah. Then she said, "Hello, Dixie."

"Hello, Zilla. I'm glad to know you." She noted that the girl was not wearing a robe like her mother's but a garment much briefer that left her arms free. She wore sandals, and her hair was very black, like Aimee's.

"My other children are not here," Fatima said. "You will meet them later, perhaps."

"You speak very good English," Sarah remarked.

"We have tried to learn your language well. We do not speak it as well as Aimee, though."

At that point the sheikh walked in, and the servants bowed deeply. He gestured toward the plastic cloth spread on the tent floor. "We will have our meal now," he announced.

Dixie and Sarah sat down quickly where Fatima indicated, and then the sheikh took his place, sitting cross-legged. His wife saw to it that trays of food were brought in. She took them from the servants and placed them before the guests first.

"You will, perhaps, not like our food," Sheikh Omar said, setting his piercing dark eyes on them.

"Oh, I'm sure we will," Sarah said quickly. "What was served us last night was delicious. And I must apologize—we are not familiar with your customs, and we don't want to offend you in any way."

Sheikh Omar stared at her and said nothing. Then, suddenly, he began to pray in Arabic.

Dixie and Sarah bowed their heads and prayed their own prayer.

"I suppose you are Christians?" Sheikh Omar said abruptly.

"Yes, we are." Sarah nodded.

"Then my daughter has told you that I do not approve of her leaving the true religion."

"Yes, she has told us."

Omar apparently expected an argument, but Sarah remained silent. He sat stiff and unbending. "She has left my house and my religion. To me she is dead."

"Do not say so, husband," Fatima said softly. She set a tray of food before him. "She is our daughter."

Her influence seemed to calm down Sheikh Omar somewhat.

Dixie even thought he looked with affection at his wife. *He really loves her*, Dixie thought. *You can see it in his eyes. But he sure is hard.*

The meal consisted of melon, dates, fresh pita bread, and a kind of sweet cake. There was also goat's milk and water, and Dixie chose the water. Goat's milk was too rich and strong for her.

As they ate, the sheikh said, "Tell me how you met my daughter."

"Yes, Sheikh Omar. It was this way . . ."

Dixie watched the sheikh's face as her aunt explained how they had become acquainted with Aimee. She noticed that he did not smile.

When Sarah finished, he picked up a date and put it in his mouth. Finally, he looked across at his wife and said, "She will not be happy. This is her home. We are her family. She should have stayed here."

"She misses you all very much, and she loves you very much," Dixie piped up. "She misses Sandy too."

Instantly Dixie sensed she had said the wrong thing, for Sheikh Omar's face clouded over. "That white camel! I hate that beast! He is a bad omen—he had something to do with my daughter's disobedience and rebellion!"

Sarah did not argue, but she did say, "Your daughter is a very loving young woman, sir. I'm sure she didn't want to displease you."

"Then why did she leave my house?"

"She has found peace with Jesus Christ."

"Muhammad was a prophet, a great prophet," Omar said. "Why could she not have been satisfied with that?"

Dixie saw that her aunt was desperately trying to avoid an argument. "I do not know your daughter's heart, but I know she is very grieved that you are displeased with her."

Sheikh Omar studied Aunt Sarah. His face was still, and Dixie could not tell what he was thinking. Abruptly, without another word, he got up and left the tent.

Fatima now sat down across from Dixie and Sarah. "You must forgive my husband. He loves Aimee very much."

Sarah nodded. "I can see that in his eyes."

"But he is a very proud man. He has never been able to admit that he's been wrong."

"That isn't good," Dixie said. "I've had to admit I was wrong many times."

Then Fatima said, "Tell me more about Aimee."

"We brought you some pictures," Dixie said quickly. They had taken many pictures of Aimee and put them in a small plastic album. She brought out the album and said, "Look, here she's helping to wash off the elephants. Isn't she pretty?"

Eagerly Fatima studied each picture. She held the book with trembling hands and listened as Dixie explained each picture. When she had seen them all, she said, "My heart is heavy. Her father and I both love Aimee very much. Be patient with him."

Dixie waited for her aunt to tell Fatima why they had come. But Sarah didn't.

When they were alone, she asked, "Why didn't you tell Aimee's mother that we're praying for God to do something to her father's heart?"

"That might not be best to say right now. Maybe later," Sarah said.

Later that day Zilla asked Dixie, "Would you like to see the animals?"

"Oh, yes," Dixie said. "Let me get my helmet on." She put on the sun hat and then squirted some sunscreen into her hands.

As she spread it on her face, Zilla said, "What's that?"

"It's to keep me from getting sunburned."

Zilla was inquisitive. "Could I have some?"

Dixie laughed. "Of course. You don't really need it though. You have beautiful olive skin."

"Olive skin?" Zilla was puzzled. "My skin is like an olive?"

"That's what we say in America for someone who has golden brown skin like you do. It's good that God made you that way or you would burn in the hot sun here. If I went out without putting this on, I'd be burnt to a cinder."

Zilla put some on her face. "It smells good," she said.

The two girls went outside, Dixie listening as Zilla talked cheerfully. She was fascinated by the large flocks of sheep and goats.

Then Zilla said, "Do you want to see the camels?"

"I'm not very fond of camels. One spit at me."

"I like them. And my sister Aimee, she loved them. Especially Sandy."

Dixie wanted to say, "I don't like any beast that spits on me," but instead she said, "All right. Let's go look."

The camels were kept off to themselves, and there seemed to be a great many of them.

"There's Sandy right over there."

Dixie looked. It was not difficult to find Aimee's favorite, for he stood out like a white dove among a flock of blackbirds.

"He really *is* white!"

"My father doesn't like him," Zilla said, "but Aimee always loved him."

"I know. She told me."

"Do you want to pet him?"

"I guess so. I promised her I'd give him a hug. But I'm afraid he'll spit on me."

"No," Zilla promised, "he won't do that."

Dixie went reluctantly with her new friend, and when they approached the white camel he turned to stare at them. He was not fully grown but almost so. His fur was beautiful, she had to admit.

"Go up and call his name," Zilla commanded.

Hesitantly Dixie went forward and said, "Hello, Sandy."

At the word "Sandy" the camel lifted his head. He had beautiful eyes, she saw, with long eyelashes. But he moved his lips in a way that made her think she was in trouble.

"He's going to spit on me!" she cried.

"No, he's not. Sandy never spits on anybody, and he's very gentle. Go on, pet his neck."

Dixie made herself walk up to the camel. Again she said, "Sandy," and the camel lowered his head. She put her arms around his neck and gave him a squeeze. "Aimee said to give you a hug," she said.

As Dixie stepped back, Sandy made an odd noise somewhere in his throat, and it looked as if he was nodding. And then the white camel put his head on her shoulder.

"You see?" Zilla cried. "He likes people very much."

Dixie stroked the thick fur and said softly, "I wish Aimee could be here."

Sandy grunted again and made a moaning noise deep down inside.

"He misses her a lot," Zilla said. "Ever since she left, he hasn't been eating right. She raised him from when he was born."

"Yes, she told me." Dixie stroked the camel's nose, and he nibbled at her fingers. She laughed and said, "Sandy, you and I are going to be great friends!"

8
AIMEE'S FRIEND

On the second day of their visit to the desert camp, Dixie and Aunt Sarah thought Fatima appeared worried about something. Sarah said she did not want to be inquisitive, but at last she asked, "Is there something wrong?"

"Oh, it is nothing," Fatima replied rather sadly. "At least nothing that you could help with."

"What is it?" Dixie asked curiously. She had grown fond of Fatima. She thought she saw the same sweet spirit in the woman that she had seen in her daughter.

"It's just that some of my husband's sheep have gotten sick. No one seems to know why, and several of them have died."

Sarah said, "Perhaps I *could* be of some help after all. That's my job with the circus, you know—taking care of sick animals."

A startled look crossed Fatima's face. "Is that so? I did not understand that." Hope came into her eyes, but then it quickly faded. "But my husband would not receive your help. He does not have much confidence in most women."

"It wouldn't hurt to ask," Dixie said. She was thinking, *If Aunt Sarah could just help the sheikh's sheep get well, he might listen to her about other things.*

"I may not be able to help at all," Sarah admitted, "but it's possible."

Fatima said no more just then, but later in the afternoon the sheikh came striding across the sand toward them, his robe billowing out in the slight breeze. Without a greeting, he said curtly, "My wife tells me that you have had some experience with sick animals."

"Yes, I have, Sheikh Omar. I am a veterinarian for a circus."

The tall Arab seemed uncomfortable, Dixie thought—probably because he hated to be under any obligation to foreigners and especially to foreign women.

But Sarah said, "I would be glad to take

a look at your animals and see if I could do anything."

"Very well. I will have one of my servants take you."

A while later, a tall young Arab came looking for Sarah. When he found her, he bowed and said, "My name is Ahmed. My master has asked me to show you the sick animals."

"Ahmed!" Dixie piped up. She thought the young man was very handsome, indeed. He had a thin black mustache and liquid-looking brown eyes. "Are you the Ahmed who is Aimee's friend?"

Surprise washed across the young man's face. He glanced around almost guiltily, and when he saw no one near, he nodded. "You know Aimee?"

"She's the reason we're here," Aunt Sarah said. She went on to explain.

When she ended, a smile touched the lips of the young Arab, but it was a sad smile.

"I miss her," he said simply. "Ever since she has been gone, I have grieved."

"Maybe God will fix it so you can be together again."

Surprised, Ahmed stared down at Dixie. "All things are possible, I know," he said.

"Show us the sick animals, please," Aunt Sarah said.

"It is better to ride. We keep them separated from the rest of the flocks. I will have camels saddled."

"Please, Mr. Ahmed, could I ride Sandy?"

"The white camel? You *must* have been talking to Aimee. He was always her favorite."

"Yes, I've already seen him. I didn't like camels much when I came, but he seems very sweet."

"Aimee's father, the sheikh, does not like him. He believes he's a bad omen."

"What's a bad omen?" Dixie asked.

"Bad luck."

"Oh, I don't believe in rabbits' feet."

Ahmed looked at her with astonishment. "A rabbit's feet? What is that?"

"Oh, some people think that if you carry the foot of a dead rabbit in your pocket, it'll bring you good luck. But I don't think there's anything to that."

"I do not believe in that either!" Ahmed said. "I believe that God watches out for us."

Sarah smiled warmly. "Aimee told us that you were a Christian."

"A Christian doctor saved my mother's life. He told us Jesus can change the inside of a man or a woman. I called on Him, and my life has been different ever since." He paused, then looked toward the sheikh's tent. "The sheikh does believe in omens and bad luck, but I think he is wrong."

"I'm surprised he would let you stay on, your being a Christian," Sarah said. "Isn't he angry with you?"

"Yes, he is angry. And to be a Christian here is always very dangerous. But my father has been his head man for many years. He knows more than any other about the state of the flocks and the herds. Sheikh Omar feels a debt of loyalty to him. For that reason only, he lets me stay, but he does not like me."

"Well, God is able. Do you have a Bible?"

"I have a New Testament."

"I brought along several Bibles," Sarah said. "One is from Aimee. She has also written you a letter."

The eyes of the young man lit up, and he said, "When we come back, I will read the letter, and I will also read the Bible. Now I will take you to the sick animals."

Dixie was delighted to see Sandy. She was confident he would not spit on her. When she called his name, he made a rumbling in his throat and laid his head on her shoulder.

"He is well trained," Ahmed said. "All you have to do is tell him to kneel, and he will do so."

Ahmed commanded the young camel to kneel, and immediately he did.

When Dixie got into the saddle, she said, "Up," which was not the Arabic word, but he seemed to know what she meant. When he was standing upright, Sandy turned his head and nibbled gently on her knee. It tickled, and she giggled, saying, "Now, Sandy, you'll have to behave." Again Sandy rumbled in his throat, then tossed his head. He seemed pleased that Dixie was astride his back.

Dixie enjoyed her ride. It was smooth and fast.

"These are racing camels," Ahmed said. "Worth very much money."

Dixie said, "I've never seen a trained camel act. We've had elephants and seals and bears and horses at the circus but never camels. I wonder why that is?"

"I do not know," Ahmed said. "It is not because they are not intelligent. Sandy can do many tricks. Aimee taught him. She is very good with camels. I will show you some of his tricks when we get back."

When they reached the sick herd, Dixie talked with Ahmed while Sarah examined some of the sheep. He talked mostly of Aimee, things that they had done together and how much they loved each other.

He said sadly, "But she is far away now. Far across the ocean, and it may be that I will never see her again."

Dixie said, "We're praying that her father will forgive her."

"He is a very proud man. I doubt if he has ever once in his life said the simple words 'I was wrong' or 'I am sorry.'" He thought a moment. "Dixie, I think those are the hardest words to say in all the world. 'I was wrong. I am sorry.'"

Dixie said quickly, "I think you're right, Ahmed. I did a wrong thing against my aunt recently, and it was *very* hard for me to say that."

"It's even harder for a man like Sheikh Omar. He has ruled over people all his life. Never once has he had anyone over him except the more powerful sheikhs—men he hardly ever sees. It's difficult for a man like him to admit he's wrong."

"His wife is different, though."

"She is a very loving woman. Much like her daughter. She would not at all be against having her daughter come back, at least for a visit, but the sheikh never would permit that."

"Don't be too quick to say that," Dixie said. She was running her hands through Sandy's thick white fur. "God can do some surprising things." She told him some of her own experiences of seeing God provide for her miraculously.

Ahmed listened carefully. Then he said, "I am a Christian, but I am not wise in the ways of the Bible. There is no one here for me to talk to, and there are no Christian services to teach me . . ."

Dixie saw sadness in his face. "Well," she said brightly, "God's going to do something about that."

Ahmed found this amusing. "You're very sure of that, are you, Dixie?"

"Oh, yes. We're all praying for God to help Aimee, and that means helping you."

Ahmed looked off into the distance. When he looked back, there was hope in his eyes. "I know Jesus can do anything He chooses, but I did not know I could ask Him about something like this."

"You can ask him for anything as long as it's not something wrong." Dixie reached out and took his hand. "You and I will pray together. If Aimee was here, she would pray with us, but she's praying anyhow, back in the States."

Ahmed bowed his head, and Dixie prayed, "Lord, nothing is too hard for You. I ask You to make the heart of Aimee's father soft. Let him forgive Aimee, and let Aimee and Ahmed be together again. In Jesus' name."

Ahmed looked at her with respect in his eyes. "You are only a girl, but you already know more about God than I do."

"I don't know much," Dixie said. "And you'll learn very quickly when you and Aimee get together again."

"God willing, that will be soon," Ahmed said fervently. Then he saw Aunt Sarah walking toward them. "Dixie and I have been praying together," he said.

"Dixie is good at that," her aunt said.

Ahmed nodded slowly. "She is telling me that Jesus can do anything, and I am going to believe that He will."

9

IT'S NEVER WISE TO TRUST A WOMAN?

Sarah sat across from Sheikh Omar, and as she gave her report about the sheep, his face hardened into distrust.

"I have never heard of this strange disease," he said. "None of our people have ever heard of it."

"It's become quite common in parts of the United States," Sarah said patiently. She said she had been at a veterinarian's professional meeting when a veterinarian from Utah reported on a virus that was destroying sheep in the northern part of the state. She described the symptoms to Sheikh Omar, then said, "It sounds very much like the disease that is happening in my country."

"How could a disease cross the ocean?" Omar demanded. "It is impossible!"

"Not at all. Viruses are very strange things!" Sarah exclaimed. "They seem to be able to leap over enormous distances, and no one knows why." She waited then, for she had done all she could.

Omar looked over at his first lieutenant, Ahmed's father. "What say you to this, Dabir?"

Dabir was a man in late middle age. Smooth shaven and tall, he resembled his son. He stroked his chin thoughtfully and said, "I will only say, master, that none of our remedies have helped. If our visitor here knows anything at all, I think we would be wise to let her try it."

"It's never wise to trust a woman," Omar said bluntly. He glared across the rug on which they sat, seeming to expect Sarah to react angrily. But she simply waited. "Very well," he said finally, throwing up his hands, "I suppose we must try everything, or we won't have a sheep left. What shall we do?"

"If a guide could take me to a city, I think I could find the medicine to make the serum from."

"The nearest town is Afif," Omar said. "As you know, we have no vehicles here, and it is a long journey by camel."

"Then perhaps I'd better leave at once," Sarah said, getting to her feet.

"Dabir, assign a trustworthy man to go with her."

"I will go myself," Dabir said. "I think it is critical, or we will lose all our animals. Who knows? The virus might leap over to the goats—or even to the horses. Who knows with a thing like this? Only Allah knows."

That thought seemed to frighten Omar, and he said, "Go at once and spare no expense."

Sarah hurried to the tent she shared with Dixie. "I think it is important that I do this, Dixie. It might be that saving his sheep will impress the sheikh enough so that he will listen to . . . other things." Then she laughed a little. "He certainly doesn't trust women. Maybe I can change his mind about that too."

"Do you want me to come along, Aunt Sarah?" Dixie asked.

Sarah hesitated. "It would be a very hard trip for you, but I don't see anything else to do."

"I could stay with Zilla. She's been begging me to stay with her anyway."

"We will have to ask her mother. Her father might object . . ."

"Her mother wouldn't. She likes me. I'll go ask her right now while you pack."

Dixie ran through the camp, dodging the cooking fires and the stray animals. She was greeted by several who had learned to say her name, and she smiled and returned each greeting with "Hello. How are you?"

When she reached the Feyds' tent and called Zilla, both the girl and her mother came to the door.

"My Aunt Sarah has to go find some medicine for the sick sheep," she said. "Would it be all right if I stayed with you until she gets back?"

"Oh, yes. It will be all right, won't it, Mother?"

Fatima nodded, smiling. "Of course it will. You tell your aunt you will be very welcome, and we will take good care of you."

Sarah left that afternoon with Dabir. Before leaving, she leaned over and kissed Dixie, saying, "It's very important that you be on your best behavior. Don't anger Sheikh Omar in any way."

"I wouldn't do that!"

"Sometimes you get a little carried away, Dixie. Just be careful and be on your best behavior." She kissed her again and gave her a hug. "I'll be back as soon as I can."

Dixie and Zilla watched Sarah and Dabir leave on the camels. Then Zilla said, "Let's go down to the stream. We can wade in it."

The two girls went down to the small stream that supplied the oasis. On each side of it grew green grass and palm trees.

"You'd better be careful here at night. The jackals come to drink, and they can be very dangerous."

"I've never seen a jackal," Dixie said. "Maybe I could get a picture of one."

"No, they come out only at night."

"That's all right. I've got a flashbulb."

"What's a flashbulb?"

"It's a thing on a camera that lights up so you can take pictures when it's dark."

As the two girls sat dabbling their feet in the water, Dixie asked many questions about Zilla's people and their way of life.

Zilla had seen some American movies while visiting her relatives in the city, and she was very curious, too. "What's it like to grow up in America?"

"Well, first of all we go to school." She went on to describe what an American school was like. Then she asked, "Is that like your school?"

"Not very much," Zilla said, "and not everyone can go to school here. Only those who can afford it get to go. A lot of children grow up never learning to read or write at all."

"That would be sad. I love to read."

"Tell me some more about your country. The movies I saw—there were gangsters shooting people. Did you ever see one of those gangsters?"

"Oh, no," Dixie said. "That's mostly just in movies. We live in a little town. There weren't any gangsters there at all."

Zilla seemed somewhat disbelieving, but she said, "How does a woman get married in your country?"

"Well, she meets a boy, and he begins to date her."

"What is dating?"

"That's when he takes her out to eat, or they go somewhere together—like to a movie."

"And do they have to have an adult with them?"

"Oh, no," Dixie said. "Not at all."

"We do in this country. A girl wouldn't go out with a man without a chaperone." She thought a while and said, "I know many girls who got married without ever having seen the man."

Dixie stared at Zilla. "You mean you would marry someone that you hadn't seen?"

Zilla shrugged. "It happens all the time. For instance, if my father wants to make an alliance with a sheikh who lives a good distance away—and he has a son my age—our fathers would meet, and they would talk about dowries and arrangements. And then on the wedding day we would meet for the first time."

"I wouldn't like that," Dixie said. "You might not like him."

"It's the way things are here. Your ways seem very strange to me, just as ours do to you."

And then Dixie asked cautiously, "Have you ever been to a Christian service?"

"Oh, no!" Zilla seemed shocked. "My father would never permit that! That's why he's so angry at Aimee."

"I know. I wonder why he dislikes Christians so much."

"My father is Muslim, and he will never be anything else." She thought for a while again. "But he did love Aimee very much. I think he's really more hurt than angry at her."

"And she's sad that he's upset. Do you think he'll ever let her come back?"

"I don't know. He's very good to all of us. I think it nearly broke his heart when she became a Christian and ran away. It would take a miracle from Allah to put them back together again."

Dixie began telling Zilla how God had done several impossible-seeming things in her own life.

After listening, Zilla said wistfully, "It sounds wonderful. You really love Jesus, don't you?"

"Yes, I do." She hesitated, then said, "Do you love Allah?"

"I don't know. Not really, I suppose. He doesn't seem real. Is Jesus real to you?"

"Yes, He is. I've read about Him so much in the Bible and prayed to Him so much—I just know He is with me."

The two girls sat for a long time cooling

their feet in the water. Then Zilla sighed. "I would be happy for any way that my sister and my father could be happy together again."

"Jesus can do it," Dixie said eagerly. "You'll see."

The two girls arose then and walked over to visit the camels.

Sandy lifted his head as soon as Dixie came in sight, and he called to her in the curious, coarse braying sound that camels have.

She met him, and he put his head on her shoulder. She patted him and hugged him hard, saying, "Here's another hug from Aimee—and one from me, Sandy!"

10
SHEIKH OMAR GOES WRONG

Dixie and her aunt wandered along the brush fence that enclosed Sheikh Omar's sickly animals.

"Do you really think the medicine will work, Aunt Sarah?"

"Yes, I do." Sarah had returned from the city with the vaccine two days earlier and had since given shots to all the sheep. "In fact, I think they're already getting better. I believe they're going to be all right."

They went back to report to the sheikh, who listened attentively as Sarah explained. When she had finished, he said, "You think the disease will not kill them, then?"

"No, but I believe you'll need to keep a supply of this vaccine on hand. After we go home, you could have Ahmed give them the shots. I'll teach him how."

"Very well." The sheikh seemed pleased for once. He put a hand on Zilla's head. "Our visitors have done us a great service, Zilla."

He was very fond of Zilla, Dixie saw. The girl stood close as he said, "Perhaps we should give them a reward."

"We do not need a reward, Sheikh Omar!" Aunt Sarah said.

"Why don't we do something special with them?" Zilla cried. "We could go to the camel races over at Benir."

The sheikh looked up. "You probably would not be interested in such a thing as camel races . . ."

"Oh, we would!" Dixie said. "I'd love to see them race!"

"I too have never seen a camel race," Aunt Sarah put in. "If it's not too much trouble, we'd enjoy that."

"It is no trouble. I expect to win the race."

"Do you ride the camels *yourself*, Sheikh Omar?" Dixie asked.

"Yes. Even though I'm not a young man anymore, I still like to ride a fast camel." He seemed truly excited, and that evening he was more pleasant than he had ever been.

When they went to bed, Dixie said, "The sheikh was very happy about his sheep."

"Yes, he was. He still won't talk about Aimee, though."

The next morning Sheikh Omar came to find them. "We will be leaving to go to the races right away. Are you ready?"

"Yes, of course."

"It is not far from here. Ordinarily, women do not attend—but since you are foreigners, my people expect anything."

Dixie whispered to Sarah as they went to mount the camels, "What does that mean?"

"I think it means that he doesn't trust foreigners much—or expect much out of any woman. But we'll enjoy the camel races anyway."

They made the trip to where the races were held in less than half a day. They found that tents had already been set up there and a great many camels had been gathered.

"It's a little bit like a county fair," Dixie said to Zilla.

"What's a county fair?"

"Oh, back in the States once a year there is what is called a county fair. Cattle, sheep, and all kinds of animals are entered into contests, and there will be carnival rides, and—"

"What's a carnival ride?"

Dixie explained as best she could the mysteries of a carnival.

Zilla was eager to see one. "I'd give anything to ride on the Octopus," she said.

"Well, I don't know. Some people don't like it. It makes their stomach turn over."

The race area was a noisy, exciting place. It was not only a place for camel races, but there were also auctions. Dixie saw men trading back and forth, buying and selling. And then it came time for the first race.

"Look, there's your father," Dixie said. "What a beautiful camel—if a camel can be beautiful."

"Do you think camels are ugly?" Zilla asked.

"Well, I did before I came here. All I knew about them was that they were ill-tempered and stubborn and would bite people and spit on them."

"Some camels do, but there are horses like that—and other animals."

Dixie thought of the Siberian tigers.

118

She thought of some of the circus horses. "Yes, I suppose you're right. Anyway, I think *Sandy* is beautiful."

"See, they're getting ready for the start."

"And look. There's Ahmed! I didn't know *he* was going to race."

"My father has several camels entered in this race, but I hope he wins himself."

A gun went off, and the camels all started forward at a fast lope. They swept over the desert sands like ships sailing over the sea, and the air was full of cheers as men cried out for their favorites to win.

"I didn't know a camel could run so fast!"

"Only those bred for racing can," Zilla answered. "Look, look! Father's going to win!"

But Dixie said, "No, it's Ahmed! Ahmed's going to win!"

It was a very close finish, but the judges ruled that Ahmed had indeed won. He had a smile on his face—but there was no smile on the face of Sheikh Omar.

"Your father ought to be glad that his camels came in first and second," Dixie said. But she saw that the sheikh was very angry. He leaped off his camel and stalked away, leaving an attendant to take care of the animal.

"My father just doesn't like to lose, and he hardly ever does." Zilla bit her lip, saying nervously, "Sometimes he's hard to get along with after he loses a race. Mother tries to tell him it's only a race, but he doesn't see it like that."

She went to her father and took his hand. "First and second place!" she cried. "That was good, Father!"

Omar did not answer. He looked back angrily at Ahmed, and Dixie knew that he was especially angry because Ahmed was a Christian and had fallen in love with his daughter. The day seemed spoiled.

Just before the feast that followed the camel racing, Ahmed came by. "I shouldn't have let my camel win. I know how much Sheikh Omar likes to be first."

"A man should do the very best he can, Ahmed," Sarah said calmly. "Surely Sheikh Omar realizes that."

"In most things he does, but he's very proud of his camels—and of his riding. It would have been better if I had held my camel back."

"That wouldn't have been honest," Dixie said. "Christians are supposed to be honest."

Ahmed reached out and touched her hair. "You are right. We will trust God to do what must be done."

All the next day Sheikh Omar was in a bad mood. He even snapped at Zilla once, which was almost unheard of. From time to time his wife tried to calm him down, but he seemed very disturbed. Late that afternoon, he shocked all of them.

Dixie and Zilla were at the camel herd. Dixie was feeding Sandy some sweet that she had brought from the table, and he was grunting and nuzzling her.

Sheikh Omar walked by with his head high and a scowl on his face. "That white camel is the cause of all my trouble! He's bad luck!"

"Oh, no, Sheikh Omar!" Dixie cried. "He's not bad luck! He's a fine camel!"

But suddenly he became very angry. "I will not have that beast in my camp!" He turned to Dabir, who was, as usual, at his right hand. "Get rid of that camel, Dabir! The white one!"

Even Dabir seemed shocked. "But he was Aimee's favorite—"

It was the wrong thing to say. The sheikh shouted, "Did you hear what I told you? *Get rid of it!*"

"You mean sell him?" Dabir asked, still confused.

"No, I mean have him destroyed! Shoot him! Have one of the men take him out in the desert and shoot him!"

Dixie's heart rose to her throat. Sandy was nuzzling her, and she held onto him with both hands. "Please," she said, "don't shoot him!"

But the sheikh only gave her a harsh look, then walked away, saying to Dabir, "You heard my orders! Do it at once!"

"Please, can't we do something?" Dixie begged.

Dabir shook his head. "There's nothing I can do." He seemed very sad, and he touched Sandy's neck gently. "He is a fine camel. It breaks my heart—but I must obey the master." He took hold of the leather halter and led Sandy away.

The camel looked back and gave his odd, grunting cry to Dixie. It was as if he was begging her to do something, but Dixie could do nothing but stand and watch.

She felt sick. She went to tell Sarah what had happened. "I love that camel! He's so sweet. Not at all like I thought a camel would be."

Sarah herself seemed shocked by the sheikh's action. She said, "I'm sorry, Dixie. I'm so sorry."

"I hate Sheikh Omar!" Dixie cried.

"You mustn't say that! That's the one thing you mustn't do! Remember," Sarah said, "Jesus tells us to love those who despitefully use us. Do you remember?"

"I remember, but he's so mean!"

"I think he's very unhappy. He loved Aimee more than you love Sandy, and he thinks he has lost her. He's very hurt and upset, so he strikes out at Sandy because Aimee loved him."

"Well, I think it's awful."

"It *is* terrible, but the sheikh is confused, and he's going to feel very bad about this in the days to come."

Dixie never asked about Sandy, but in the next two days she noticed that Sheikh Omar did become unusually attentive. He never mentioned the camel, but Zilla said, "He feels bad. I know he does."

It was too late, though. Dixie thought, *We can never take the white camel to Aimee now.*

Sarah said, "I should write her. It's going to be hard to tell her that her favorite camel is dead. And especially that her father had him killed."

"I'm not sure we should *ever* tell her that. Maybe she won't ever ask."

The next day Zilla came rushing to their tent. "Miss Sarah, my father's favorite horse! He's broken his leg, and they're going to shoot him!"

"Oh, how awful!"

Dixie and Aunt Sarah went at once with Zilla. The horse had fallen while he was being exercised. He was lying on the ground, and Sheikh Omar was standing beside him, a grieved look on his face.

Sarah knelt beside the animal, saying, "Can you hold him still while I look at his leg?"

"There is no need looking. His leg is broken. He must be shot." Sheikh Omar's voice was harsh, but there was pain in his dark eyes.

Aunt Sarah felt the leg carefully as the men held the horse down. Then she looked up and said, "It isn't a bad break, Sheikh Omar. We can put a splint on him and rig a harness so that he can't put much weight on it. I think he'll be all right."

Sheikh Omar swallowed hard. "That cannot be. There is no cure for a broken leg."

"If they are very badly broken, that's probably true, but this is more a crack than a break. If you'll have your men help me, I'll make a splint. Then we can put him on a harness under one of the trees over there so that for a few days he won't have to put weight on it."

Sheikh Omar began barking orders, and soon Sarah had devised a splint, and the injured horse was standing in a harness that held most of his weight off the ground.

Sheikh Omar said, "See that he has food and water." Then he turned to Sarah, his eyes bright. "Do you really think he will be all right?"

"I don't see why not, Sheikh Omar. I've done this many times back in my country."

Dixie was thinking, *He always said it's foolish to trust a woman. Let's see what he says now.*

Two days later Omar approached Aunt Sarah and said, "My horse is much better."

"I'm so pleased to hear it. He's a fine animal, but he needs to stay in the harness for at least another two days."

"It shall be as you say." The sheikh stood studying Aunt Sarah. He said, "I am most grateful, for, as you know, I love that horse more than any of the others."

Sarah smiled. "I'm glad I was able to help."

"I would like to give you a reward."

"Sir, your hospitality is enough. I wouldn't take any pay."

"I was not thinking of money," Sheikh Omar said. He kept his eyes fixed on her as he said, "I will find some other way to repay you, for I am very grateful." He turned and walked away.

Dixie said, "Well, he's learned to trust women—at least one woman anyhow."

Sarah watched the sheikh's departure. "And he loves his daughter more than he loves that horse. Maybe this will soften him."

11
THE MIDDLE
OF NOWHERE

The time of departure was drawing near for Sarah and Dixie. More than once Dixie had thought she had seen a break in the hardness of Sheikh Omar Feyd, and it encouraged her. She certainly saw that he was kind to his family and treated well those who worked for him. However, it was also clear that he still had problems with his daughter Aimee.

Dixie and Zilla had become fast friends. Dixie had learned a great deal about the Arab countries and their people from the girl.

Dixie had brought only one of her Barbie dolls with her—Eliza, which Mickey had given her. She described her other dolls to Zilla and promised to send her one as a gift as soon as she got home.

After the last midday meal, Zilla offered

to show Dixie a spring where the antelope often came to drink. Dixie, of course, was always interested in any animal, and the two girls started off.

"Do not go too far," Zilla's mother called out. She looked at the sky and said, "It looks as if we could have a storm."

"Oh, it'll be all right, Mother," Zilla answered. She turned to Dixie and said, "She worries about me too much."

"That's the way it is with mothers. They're always worried about their children."

By the time they came near the spring, the sky was indeed growing dark. "Maybe we'd better turn back," Dixie said.

"No, it's just a little way up here. I want you to see it."

"Your mother said to be careful about storms."

"Oh," Zilla said carelessly, "in the desert these clouds come and go. They don't mean anything."

But Dixie was nervous, for the clouds behind them were black and lay low on the horizon. She kept watching as the blackness grew larger, and when they reached the spring, she said, "Zilla, I think we'd better go back. Look at that cloud."

Zilla had been chattering away, but now she turned to look behind them, and her eyes grew wide. "It's a sandstorm," she gasped, "and it's coming fast!"

The two girls started to run, but minutes later they were almost blown over as a powerful wind struck them. The sun darkened so that it was almost like night. The sand stung as it hit Dixie's face.

"Can you find your way, Zilla?"

"This sand hurts my eyes, but I think this is the way."

They fought against the wind. It shifted, and the sky grew even blacker. And then Zilla said, "I think we've made a wrong turn. We'd better turn around."

Dixie had always had a fear of being lost. She grabbed Zilla's hand and hung on as the storm howled. "I never heard such a noise," Dixie said. "It sounds like a freight train!"

"What did you say?" Zilla yelled.

"Nothing!" Dixie said. "Let's just hurry!"

It was obvious that Zilla had lost her sense of direction, and on the desert there were few landmarks. They saw no tents. For all Dixie knew, they were headed directly *away* from the camp. And the sandstorm did not get better but worse.

131

"Dixie," Zilla gasped, "we're going to have to find shelter."

There was little shelter on the desert, either, but they did come to a small gully. The bottom was filling with sand, but at least they could get out of the full blast of the wind.

"I'm afraid," Zilla whimpered. "People get lost in these sandstorms, and the storms last for days sometimes."

"Your father will find us."

"But no one can track us because the sand blows all our tracks away." She held tightly to Dixie's hand and shut her eyes. Her lips were trembling.

Dixie was frightened herself. With more confidence than she felt, she said, "It'll be all right. When the storm blows over, they'll send somebody out to look for us."

The two girls clung together, while the wind howled and screamed. More than once they had to brush away the sand that was rapidly filling their trench.

Dixie wondered, *What will we do if it keeps on like this all night? We'll be buried alive!* Still, she was sure of one thing: *Jesus knows where we are.* She began to pray that the Lord would send someone to find them.

"This is awful!" Sarah exclaimed. She stood clasping her hands tightly together. The sheikh's tent was being shaken by the powerful wind blasts. "We've got to do something!"

Sheikh Omar Feyd's face was tense. "As soon as the wind dies down, I will send men out in every direction. No one can go out now." He turned to his wife. "Did the girls say which way they were going?"

"No, just that they were going out for a walk."

"Which way were they headed?"

"That way," Fatima whispered. Fear was in her eyes, and she glanced upward as the storm clawed like a beast at the tent fabric. "Can't we go now, Omar?"

"You know it would be useless." The sheikh began to pace the tent carpeting. "We must wait until the wind dies down. There are no tracks to follow." And desperation was in his voice.

Sarah was terrified. All this was beyond her experience. She only knew that Dixie and her friend Zilla were in terrible danger. She too began to walk slowly back and forth, praying.

The time passed very slowly, and the wind seemed to increase in velocity.

Sarah looked up when Ahmed stumbled into the tent. Wiping the sand out of his eyes, he said, "Master, I tried to go out, but it is not possible. Not until the wind dies down." He turned to Sarah and said, "I did my best, Miss Logan."

"I know you did," Sarah said. She touched his arm and tried to smile. "No one could do anything in a storm like this."

"Perhaps they will find a place to hide until the storm is over," Ahmed said hopefully.

"Where would they hide?" Sheikh Omar moaned. "There's not even a tree to hide behind in that direction. They have no protection, no water, no food, nothing!"

Sarah took a deep breath. "I know this seems very hard. It does to me too. We love these children, all of us, but right now it's out of our hands."

"That is true," Sheikh Omar said, bowing his head and staring at the carpet. "It is all in the hands of Allah."

"It is in the hands of our loving God," Sarah said. "It's at times like these we must remember that God is able to do anything."

The sheikh looked up. "Your God or my God?"

"There is only one God, Sheikh Omar,

and His Son is Jesus Christ." After a few seconds, she said, "God created this earth. You know that is what the Scriptures say. Now we must ask Him who created both the earth and the two girls who are lost to care for them. With God all things are possible."

Fatima was sobbing softly. She was standing beside her husband, and he put his arm around her.

"Jesus will find them," Sarah said. She saw unbelief in the sheikh's eyes and knew that he had lost hope. But she herself suddenly felt that God was very close. She began to pray aloud as if she spoke to an earthly father.

"Oh, Lord, You know these children. You knew them before they were born. Now, Lord, their safekeeping is out of our hands, and I ask You in the name of Jesus— keep them safe and then guide us to them. I ask this is the name of Jesus of Nazareth."

A silence fell over the tent, broken only by the roaring of the wind. Sarah did not look up. She did not know how her prayer had affected the proud man who had never begged for anything. She only knew that it was the only thing that could be done.

12
A SANDSTORM VISITOR

The night was blacker than Dixie could have imagined possible. The wind howled. Every star was blotted out. She looked up, shielding her eyes from the blowing sand, and could see nothing at all. She shut them quickly, huddled back beside Zilla, and whispered, "Don't cry. We'll be all right."

"We will die out here in the desert."

"God won't let us die," Dixie said confidently.

The wind became even more fierce. It was all Dixie could do to keep her hands pressed against her face. She felt the sand piling into the trench on top of them. She was very thirsty.

It was the longest night Dixie had ever experienced, and the longer she lay there, the more thirsty she grew. *I'd give any-*

thing for a drink of water, she thought desperately. *I didn't realize how good just plain water would be. Better than a milkshake, or a Pepsi, or a Coke.*

Time passed, and finally the screaming wind seemed to be dying down.

"I think the wind's not blowing as hard, Zilla," she said.

Zilla lifted her head. Sand was in her hair and on her face. She brushed it away. "We can never find our way back, and if we don't get water soon, I don't know what will happen."

"Your father will find us," Dixie promised.

"There are no *tracks*. And they don't have any idea where we are. Besides, they can't start looking till the storm's gone."

Dixie could not comfort Zilla much, for she was frightened herself. She set her mind to thinking about familiar things— about Aunt Sarah, about her parents in Africa, about the animals she had loved— Jumbo and Stripes and Dolly. She thought about Mickey and how the two of them had prayed for Aimee. The thought of his red hair and blue eyes cheered her up. Finally she dozed off.

Dixie dreamed. She saw a white camel

out in the desert. The dream was just one quick flash, almost like a single picture, and when she woke up and brushed more sand away from her face, she said aloud, "That was Sandy I dreamed about."

In the east, light began to appear on the horizon.

"The wind's almost quit blowing, and it's almost daylight," Dixie announced.

The girls got to their feet.

"It may start to blow again," Zilla said. "It does that sometimes. It lies down like a wild beast to rest, and then it gets worse again."

"Zilla," Dixie said, "we've got to find our way back to camp. Which way do you think it is?"

Zilla looked around in despair. The desert was swept clean of anything familiar. New dunes had been formed. It looked nothing at all like the country they had come through. "I don't know."

"Can you make a guess?"

"Maybe . . . maybe that way."

"Come on, then." Dixie started off in the direction Zilla pointed. "We've got to do something."

The sun was soon up, and Dixie had

never been so thirsty in all her life. Her tongue felt swollen, and her lips were dry and chapped. Also she had only a little unused sunscreen in her pocket. Soon she had used this up.

The heat grew fierce, and before long the girls were staggering.

Zilla said, "We've got to get out of the sun."

Dixie looked around them in search of shelter. "Aren't those bushes over there?"

"I think so."

The bushy growth was no more than three feet high, but by crawling into it they were screened somewhat from the blazing sun. They lay there in the semishade, panting, too exhausted to speak.

Dixie once again thought of home and her parents. She dozed off, dreaming of her early childhood when she would ride on her father's shoulders and he would throw her high in the air.

She slept, but she tossed about. Her skin burned. And then it seemed that something wet touched her cheek.

I was dreaming, Dixie thought, but then she realized that something *was* touching her cheek. Reaching out without opening her eyes, she felt something furry and soft.

"Sandy!" she cried and struggled to her feet.

Her cry awakened Zilla, who came to a sitting position. She too cried out when she saw the camel.

"Sandy, I thought you were dead!" Dixie threw her arms around him, and he nudged her with his nose. "I don't understand," she said. "Your father sent him off to be shot."

"I know," Zilla said suddenly. "Our people love camels. The man was tenderhearted and just took him out and turned him loose. He hasn't been shot. He's fine."

Dixie was still hugging Sandy. She was almost crying, she was so relieved to see him.

"He'll take us home, Dixie!" Zilla said. "Let's get on his back."

"Kneel," Dixie said in Arabic. There was no saddle, and when Zilla got on behind her, they had to cling to the white fur. Dixie said, "Home, Sandy! Go home!"

Zilla said, "That's not the word for 'home' that he knows." She called out an Arabic word, and at once the camel got up and began to lope across the desert floor.

"Don't camels get sand in their eyes? Mine are full of it," Dixie said.

"They've got an extra eyelid. They can close it to keep the sand out."

"I wish I had one," Dixie said.

The two girls clung to the camel as he cantered smoothly across the dunes. The sun was still hot, and Dixie knew she was burning. But then Sandy suddenly stopped and lowered his head, she heard the sound of water and opened her eyes. "Water, Zilla! It's a little oasis."

The two girls came off the camel and began to drink from the spring. "The Bible says there'd be streams in the desert," Dixie said gratefully when she had drunk all she dared. "I believe God put this spring here for us."

Zilla checked the position of the sun. "Perhaps we're not too far from home," she said. "And Sandy knows the way. Let's get on his back again."

At their command, the white camel resumed racing across the dunes. It was all Dixie could do to hold on. But after what seemed a long time, she heard something familiar. Lifting her head, she managed to open her gritty eyes. "Zilla, it's your camp! Sandy brought us home!"

Sarah was there waiting when Dixie fell off the white camel. She seized her with a fierce hug. "You're safe! God has brought you back!"

"God sent Sandy to save us, Aunt Sarah."

Sheikh Omar Feyd was holding his daughter, as tears rolled down his cheeks. They were speaking in Arabic, but Zilla kept pointing to Sandy.

The sheikh had been gazing down at his daughter, but then he looked at Dixie. Next he looked at the white camel. He walked toward Sandy and held out his hand. The camel touched it with his nose, and Sheikh Omar Feyd said the words that none of his family or employees had ever heard him say. "I was wrong, and I am sorry. The white camel was sent by Allah. He is not bad luck."

Dixie felt tears rise in her eyes.

"We've got to get something on your skin. You're badly burned," Aunt Sarah said.

When Dixie tried to walk, Aunt Sarah almost had to hold her up because she was so weak.

When her burning skin was coated with cool, soothing ointment, she smiled up at her aunt. "The sheikh is changing."

"I think he is. I think God used that white camel to start bringing him to his senses."

"Do you think he'll forgive Aimee?"

"With God—" Sarah smiled, then leaned over and kissed Dixie "—with God all things are possible."

13

SHEIKH OMAR CALLS A MEETING

It was their final night in the camp of Sheikh Omar Feyd.

"I'm disappointed in the sheikh," Dixie said. She was fixing her hair, which was full of snarls. She had very thick hair, and the desert climate dried it out and made it harder to deal with.

"Why are you disappointed with Sheikh Omar?" Aunt Sarah asked. She studied her face in a small mirror and added a bit of lipstick. Then she looked at Dixie.

"He hasn't said a word more about Sandy. You would think he'd be grateful enough to *say* something. After all, Sandy saved his daughter's life—and mine too."

"I've wondered about that myself."

Before Sarah could say more, a servant

appeared at the tent door. He said something in Arabic, then motioned for them to come.

"Looks like it's time to go to the supper," she said. She had put on a long, cool dress. It was ankle length and made of pale blue cotton gauze. Dixie also wore a dress, which felt odd after wearing slacks all this time.

Evening was coming on, and stars began to spangle the heavens. All signs of the sandstorm were gone, and Dixie's sunburn was doing well.

Sheikh Omar welcomed them to his tent. Several people were already present, and Dixie was startled to see Ahmed among them.

"These are some of my other children," the sheikh said. He introduced his two sons and an older woman and her husband. Dixie could not pronounce their names, but they were all handsome people.

Sheikh Omar said, "We are honored to have our guests from America, and now we will eat."

The feast offered delicacies that Dixie had not tasted before. She did not know what everything was, though she was relatively sure that the meat was goat. However, she did not have much appetite. As she sat on the rug beside her aunt, Dixie was still feeling very disappointed. She was thinking, *We did all we knew how to do, but it looks like we failed.*

When the feast was over, Sheikh Omar stood, saying, "Since not all of my family speaks English, I will speak in both English and in my own language. I will interpret myself," which was what he did. He would say a phrase in English, then repeat it in Arabic.

"I have always been a proud man," he said. "This is good in some respects. All men and women—and young people—" here he looked at Dixie and Zilla "—must take pride in themselves. They must never be less than the very best. This is the way my father and mother brought me up."

The guests listened quietly as the sheikh continued. "I have often made remarks about women." He smiled then at Sarah. "I believe I said once in your hearing that it is not wise to trust a woman's judgment. I must tell you that I am sorry I ever said such a thing."

He turned to Fatima. "My wife certainly is a wise woman."

Dixie smiled broadly at Fatima and received a smile back. It seemed that the woman knew something, for she appeared happier than Dixie had ever seen her. Dixie turned her attention back to the sheikh.

He looked at both Sarah and Dixie, saying, "I did not welcome you properly when you came to my home. I was too filled with unforgiveness toward my daughter, and I was not a good host. I did not want to hear about Aimee, not because I hated her, but because I had such love for her in my heart."

He bowed his head to stare at the carpet. When he lifted his eyes, he looked directly at his American guests. "I was wrong about my daughter. If I had been a wiser man, I would have been more kind. When you go back to America, you must tell my daughter some things. We will give you letters, but some things are better said with the lips." He seemed to be waiting for a reply.

"We will be happy to carry any message, sir," Aunt Sarah said.

"You will tell her that her father loves

her, and he no longer has any hardness in his heart. She is welcome to come back to this place anytime."

He paused, and his wife whispered something in his ear.

"My wife reminds me that other things must be said." He turned to Ahmed, who sat at the end of the line of guests and now looked shocked as the sheikh said, "Tell my daughter Aimee that she has my permission to marry Ahmed and that one of my wedding gifts to them will be the white camel."

Dixie could no longer restrain herself. She jumped up and clapped wildly. Then she saw everyone staring, and she put her hand over her mouth. "Oh, I'm sorry!" she said.

"Do not be sorry, my little friend," the sheikh said. "It is good to see such joy. You may tell my daughter that the white camel will be on the way with her beloved—along with five other camels." He smiled then. "In her letter she says that they will make the name of Omar Feyd famous in all of America. The Famous Feyd Camel Troupe. Is it not so?"

"I think it is so, Sheikh Omar," Sarah

said. "There are no trained camels in America, and, indeed, after your son-in-law and your daughter train them, they *will* be famous and your name will be known, as you say, all over America."

As soon as Omar Feyd translated this, there was loud applause from the others, and all the guests stood.

Then the sheikh went to Zilla and held her tightly. His wife came to his side, and he put his free arm around her.

"Tell Aimee," he said quietly, "that her father and her mother and her brothers and her sisters love her and long to see her."

Dixie felt Sarah's arm tighten around her. "We will tell her, Sheikh Omar. She loves you, too."

"Take the white camel, then. He found favor in your eyes, did he not, Dixie?"

"Yes!"

"Then I am content. I will have my daughter back."

And now for the first time in America we give you the famed trained camels of Sheik Omar Feyd. The directors of the camels will be Ahmed and Aimee."

The lights came on at the center of the Big Top, and Dixie watched with excitement as Sandy plodded into the tent, leading a troupe of five camels. They were very impressive, for they all wore gold and silver harness and gear. Sandy led proudly with his head held high.

"Hooray for Sandy!" Dixie yelled.

Aunt Sarah and Mickey, standing beside her, both cheered for the white camel.

Their act was simple, but the spectators loved it.

When Ahmed and Aimee brought the camels outside the ring, Dixie met them.

She reached up and hugged Sandy. "It was wonderful!" she said and received a hug from both trainers.

Aimee and Ahmed had been married soon after he had arrived in the States, and then, after a brief honeymoon, they had begun to work with the camels.

"Your father will be very proud, Aimee," Aunt Sarah said. "We must send him pictures."

Ahmed looked both proud and happy. "We owe you two much," he said to Aunt Sarah and Dixie. Then he put an arm around Aimee. "One day we will go back to your home, Aimee. Then how happy your parents will be! And not just to see you."

"Because of the famous act of the famous camels of Sheikh Omar Feyd?" Aunt Sarah asked.

"No, because she has such a handsome husband."

They all laughed, and then Dixie left to do her act with the tiger.

Finally the time came for the grand parade. This time the six camels lined up to participate.

Dixie saw Eric and Darla laughing about something.

"What are you laughing about?" she asked.

Eric could not contain himself. "I gave that white camel some tobacco, and he's chewing it. Why, he's just a big old tobacco worm!"

Darla was laughing, too. She was wearing a pure white dress with silver threads, and she looked beautiful. "He's such an ugly thing. Look at him chew that tobacco!"

But suddenly Sandy decided he did not like tobacco. He spit a thick stream of tobacco juice. It struck Darla Castle in the face. It ran down the front of her white dress. She screamed.

Then Sandy turned and spit the remainder of the juice all over Eric. He yelled and fled.

Dixie began to laugh. "They're both going to miss the parade," she told Mickey, "but I couldn't help laughing. They just looked so funny."

"Served them right," Mickey said. He was laughing, too.

Dixie put her arms around Sandy, and he laid his head on her shoulder. There was a little tobacco juice on his lips, but he was not spitting anymore.

"Come on, Sandy. Let's do the Spec, then afterwards I'll get you something better than tobacco."

Sandy knelt, and Dixie got on. This time she was going to ride a camel in the parade. "Come on, Mickey—you can ride a horse anytime, but you can't ride a white camel that's a hero to all America."

"Right on!" Mickey said, and he scrambled up behind her.

As Dixie felt his hands lock in front of her, she commanded Sandy to rise. The tent flap opened, and the parade started. "Hold on tight," she cried as Sandy swung along. Then she yelled, "Not that tight! You're going to squeeze me in two!"

"Just getting in practice. When you get older, maybe I'll do this a lot."

Dixie said, "If you do, I'll have Sandy spit tobacco juice all over you."

They entered the Big Top then, and as the performers paraded around the track, there were cheers. Dixie and Mickey waved frantically.

Dixie patted the camel's neck. "Good for you, Sandy," she said. She knew she would always love the white camel. He had saved her life and Zilla's life. And now as they swung along, she said, "You're a good old white camel, you are."